A NEW SKATING DRESS

"I really wish you would make the effort to be pleasant to Roger," Mrs. Carsen said. "You can be so charming when you want to be." She tucked a stray curl of hair behind Tori's ear. "Please, I'm asking you for me, just try a little."

"I *am* trying," Tori lied. Then she thought of something. "Hey, Mom," she said, "what about my dress? The competition is in less than two weeks. What if you can't get it done in time?"

"Tori, you know that getting my designs into Roger's store is a major opportunity for me," Mrs. Carsen explained. She sighed. "Frankly, your dress is not top priority right now. But I'll do my best."

Tori couldn't believe her ears. "M-Mom," she sputtered, "you *told* me you were going to make me a dress for Rochester! I can't believe this. It's all because of that stupid Roger Arnold!"

CENTER ICE

Melissa Lowell

Created by Parachute Press

A SKYLARK BOOK

NEW YORK • TORONTO • LONDON • SYDNEY • AUCKLAND

RL 5.0, 009-012
CENTER ICE
A Skylark Book / June 1995

Skylark Books is a registered trademark of Bantam Books,
a division of Bantam Doubleday Dell Publishing Group, Inc.
Registered in U.S. Patent and Trademark Office and elsewhere.
Series design: Barbara Berger

ISBN 0-553-48313-7

Published simultaneously in the United States and Canada

Bantam Books are published by Bantam Books, a division of Bantam Doubleday Dell Publishing Group, Inc. Its trademark, con-
sisting of the words "Bantam Books" and the portrayal of a
rooster, is Registered in U.S. Patent and Trademark Office and in
other countries. Marca Registrada. Bantam Books, 1540 Broad-
way, New York, New York 10036.

PRINTED IN THE UNITED STATES OF AMERICA

OPM   0   9   8   7   6   5   4   3   2   1

1

"So, do you think you'll have your new routine done in time for the Rochester competition, Tori?" asked Danielle Panati.

Tori Carsen nodded to her friend. "Blake's almost finished teaching it to me now." Her blue eyes sparkled. "I'm so excited. My mom said she'd make me a new skating dress for it, too. In fact, she's supposed to show me some sketches tonight. I can't wait to see what she's come up with."

It was Monday afternoon and the members of Silver Blades, one of the country's most exclusive figure skating clubs, had just finished practice. Haley Arthur and Nikki Simon unlaced their skates on the bench next to Tori and Danielle.

"A new dress—that's great, Tori," said Haley, smiling. "But remember, it's still the *skating* that counts."

"Why am I not surprised that you would say that, Haley?" Tori replied with a laugh. She shook her head. "Miss Tomboy U.S.A. You'd probably be happy skating in a paper bag as long as you and Patrick did a perfect star-lift."

All four girls laughed at the idea of Haley and her pairs skating partner, Patrick McGuire, dressed in paper bags.

Haley definitely wasn't into frills, but she did have her own cool style. Although Tori would never dress that way herself, she thought Haley looked good in her black jeans, scuffed sneakers, oversized flannel shirt, and one earring. And she definitely admired Haley's dedication to skating. Haley and Patrick had been practicing hard the skating routine that Blake Michaels had choreographed for them.

Tori brushed a blond curl out of her eyes as she leaned over to tuck her skates into her bag. She spotted Blake across the rink demonstrating a flawless double axel for some of the Silver Blades skaters, and she sighed. It was great working with Blake on her new routine, even though he was a demanding instructor. Not only was Blake a talented ice dancer and a good choreographer, but with his dark hair and blue eyes, he was incredibly handsome, too.

Ever since he had come to Silver Blades several months earlier, Tori had had a crush on him. The trouble was, at thirteen, Tori was at least ten years younger than Blake. She could tell that he thought of her as just a kid. She only hoped that her mom would make her a truly beautiful outfit for the competition, something as dazzling as Blake's choreography. Then Blake would be really proud of her.

Haley's voice cut into her thoughts. "So, Nikki," Haley said, "you must be pretty psyched about the new baby."

"I can't wait," Nikki said excitedly. "My mom is due in just over two weeks! And I *know* it's going to be a girl. Can you believe it? I'm going to be a big sister!"

Nikki's green eyes sparkled under her brown bangs. It had taken her a little while to get used to the idea, but now Nikki seemed to look forward to having a baby sister—or brother.

Tori couldn't imagine what it would be like to have a new member of the family. At the Carsen house, it had always been Tori and her mom, as long as she could remember. Tori barely even knew her father, who had left her mother when Tori was only six months old.

Nikki rummaged through her bag. "Anybody hungry?" she asked, ripping the wrapper off a chocolate chip granola bar.

"*Very!*" said Danielle. "But chocolate's off-limits if I'm going to keep my weight down for Rochester." She sighed. "You're so lucky, Nikki. You can eat anything you want. Me—I *look* at food and gain weight." Danielle searched her backpack. "I think I have an apple here someplace," she muttered.

With her honey-brown hair and dark brown eyes, Danielle was pretty, but she had a somewhat stocky build. She was always watching her weight. She glumly took a bite of her apple.

"Hey, you're doing great, Dani," said Haley. "Besides, an apple a day keeps the doctor away. Think about how good and healthy you feel." She turned to Nikki. "But Nikki, what's all this about a *sister*? Wouldn't it be fun to have a brother you could play with, go to ball games with, go hiking with, or do any of that cool stuff?"

"Like I said—Miss Tomboy U.S.A.!" Tori teased, and the others laughed.

Tori knew that Haley didn't mind her teasing. Haley had a great sense of humor and loved pulling practical jokes on her friends. But sometimes her tricks got her into trouble.

"Oh, a brother would be fine, don't get me wrong," said Nikki, finishing off her granola bar and zipping her skating bag. "I'll be happy no matter what the baby turns out to be. But a little sister would be so much fun!" She got up from the bench. "Ready to go, guys?"

Tori looked questioningly at Danielle. "Do you think your grandmother is here yet?" she asked hesitantly.

"We probably have to wait about ten more minutes," Danielle answered. "She likes to have dinner ready before she leaves to pick me up. No wonder I have a hard time dieting with a grandmother like her. We're having her special spaghetti sauce tonight. *Yum.*" Danielle's stomach growled, and all the girls burst into giggles.

"You better get going, Dani. Dinner is coming in loud and clear," joked Nikki. "But why are *you* taking Tori home?"

"Her mom's not here today," Danielle answered.

Tori's friends looked surprised.

Everybody in Silver Blades knew Mrs. Carsen was completely involved in Tori's skating career. Tori's mom had dreams for Tori—big dreams. She'd practically had a fit when Jill Wong, another member of Silver Blades, had been chosen over Tori to attend the prestigious International Ice Academy in Denver. Tori had been jealous of Jill, too, but happy for her friend as well. Now that Jill was back in Seneca Hills with a serious injury to her ankle, Tori truly felt bad for her. How terrible not to know if you'll ever skate again, she thought.

Tori knew that if an injury like that ever happened to her, her mother would probably feel worse than she did. That Mrs. Carsen wasn't at practice today, calling to Tori from the sidelines, pushing her to do her best, was really unusual. Mrs. Carsen's loud raspy voice was a familiar sound to the Silver Blades skaters. Too familiar, Tori often thought. But today her mom had an important meeting with Roger Arnold, of Arnold's Department Stores.

"Where's your mom, Tori?" Haley asked.

"My mom is very busy right now. She's got a lot of

fashion sketches she needs to finish by the end of the week," Tori answered.

Tori didn't feel like talking about her mother's meeting with Mr. Arnold. This was the fourth meeting they'd had in the past two weeks, and Tori wasn't happy about it. Sure she was glad that her mother had this great opportunity to sell her clothing designs, but she didn't see why her mom and Mr. Arnold had to spend *so* much time together. Mrs. Carsen had never done this for any of her other clients.

Tori picked up her bag and shrugged on her bright blue parka. She followed the girls around the rink to the big swinging doors that led outside.

"I noticed it was quiet today, but I didn't realize it was because your mom wasn't here," Nikki blurted. She blushed as soon as she said it. "Oh, I didn't mean it like that, Tori. It's great that your mom cares so much about your skating," Nikki said quickly. "Is she working on your dress? Is that why she wasn't here today?"

"Of course she's working on my dress," Tori snapped. "I told you she's showing me the sketches tonight."

Tori was upset about her mother's missing practice. She had to admit, though, that it was nice for once to skate without her mom barking criticism every five minutes. Tori talked a lot with Blake and giggled with her friends. It was fun, but she felt weird. Practice was supposed to be hard work.

Tori realized she had hurt Nikki's feelings and tried to change the tone of her voice. "Actually, my mother's been working a lot with Roger Arnold. Of Arnold's Department Stores, you know? They're opening a store here in Seneca Hills. Mr. Arnold thinks my mom's fashion designs will sell really well there. So she's been working hard to get them done in time."

"Wow! Tori, why didn't you say something earlier? You must be so proud of her!" Haley exclaimed.

"Yeah," Danielle said. "Isn't Arnold's Department Stores a big national company?"

"There was one near my old house in Missouri. We used to go there all the time," Nikki said. "This could be the break your mother needs to go really big!"

"I guess," Tori said as she pulled on her gloves carefully, adjusting one finger at a time. Her new blue gloves with fake fur trim matched her parka perfectly.

"You *guess*?" Haley said incredulously. "Are you feeling all right? Is there something you're not telling us?" Haley put her hands on her hips and narrowed her eyes.

"You look like Sarge when you do that," Danielle said with a laugh. "You won't get Tori to tell you any secrets looking like a coach."

"Sarge" was the girls' nickname for Kathy Bart— Nikki and Haley's superstrict skating coach.

"Unless the coach's name is Blake, of course!" Nikki added playfully.

All the girls giggled. Tori blushed.

"You guys, Mr. Arnold is hiring my mom to do some special clothing designs for his new store, that's all. There's no secret, okay? He's originally from Seneca Hills and he wanted to use local talent. Look, Dani, isn't that your grandmother's car?" She pointed across the parking lot to the Volvo pulling up.

When Danielle nodded, Tori was relieved. For some reason, the conversation about her mother and Mr. Arnold made her uncomfortable.

On the ride home, Tori sat in front with Grandma Panati. Danielle shared the back with her brother, Nicholas, who also practiced at the rink with his hockey team. Nicholas had spiky brown hair and was in the eighth grade, a year ahead of Danielle and Tori.

"Hey, Tubs," Nicholas said to his sister, "work off any of that baby fat in practice today?"

Nicholas was only joking, but Tori knew that he often hurt Danielle's feelings. Tori felt really lucky that she never had to put up with brothers and sisters pestering her. It was one of the best things about being an only child.

"At least I don't look like I was hit in the face with a hockey puck," Danielle shot back.

"All right, you two, that's enough," said Grandma Panati. "So, Tori, tell us, what's new with you? How's your mama?"

"Tori's mom is working on some designs for the

new Arnold's Department Store," Danielle announced excitedly.

"Wow, that's a pretty big deal, isn't it?" Nicholas said. "There are signs all over the mall for that store. There's going to be some kind of grand opening or something."

"You must be so proud of your mama, Tori. It's nice that she is doing well in her business," Grandma Panati said. "When I was a girl, women didn't have the kinds of chances you do today. A good spaghetti sauce, now that was important. Do you want to come to dinner, Tori? I made my special sauce."

"Oh, thanks, Grandma Panati, I love your sauce! But my mom and I are supposed to go over sketches for my new dress tonight," Tori explained. "She's going to make me something really special for the competition in Rochester. And you know that's coming up in less than two weeks, so we have to get started."

"Oh, a new dress and new designs for a big store," said Grandma Panati. "No wonder your mama couldn't pick you up today. She's a very busy woman."

While the Panatis chatted about the day's events, Tori's attention wandered to the upcoming Rochester Competition. What if the new skating dress wasn't ready, she suddenly worried. But that would *never* happen. Her mother *always* made her a new dress for every competition. As Mrs. Carsen always said, "You've got to look like a winner to be a winner." And this time it was especially important that

Tori's dress be perfect—so Blake would notice her flawless skating.

Tori thought of Blake and how he'd want to choreograph *every* program for her. She'd be his star pupil. She smiled at the thought. Then Tori remembered the way Mrs. Carsen smiled when she talked about Mr. Arnold. Now why would I think of that, she wondered, as the car pulled up in her driveway.

"Good-bye, Dani, see you in the morning," she said, opening the car door. "Thanks for the ride, Grandma Panati. Bye, Nicholas."

She climbed out of the Volvo and waved as they drove off. As she hurried toward the side door, she wondered what was for dinner. All that talk about spaghetti sauce had made her really hungry. But as she put her key in the door, she realized something was missing. The silver Jaguar, which her mother always parked in the driveway, was not there.

But her mother was supposed to be home by now. She never stayed out this late. Where could she possibly be?

2

Tori hurried inside the dark house. "Mom? Are you here?" she called out.

No answer.

Tori started to feel a little panicked. Her mother had promised to be home right after the meeting with Mr. Arnold. Mrs. Carsen always did what she said she was going to do, and she expected Tori to do the same. It was part of what made their relationship so special—what made them a team.

So where is she? Tori worried, flicking on the lights. Then she noticed that there was a message on the answering machine. Maybe it was for her. Tori pushed "play" and leaned against the wall to listen.

"Hi, honey," came her mother's voice. "I hope you had a good practice and that you worked on those toe loops like we talked about." Tori rolled her eyes.

Her mother never let up. "That's my girl. Listen Tori, I know we were going to go over the sketches for your dress tonight, but I'm tied up in this meeting with Mr. Arnold. The store opens soon, and we had some important details about my designs to discuss, so we're working through dinner. I'm sorry, but I'll be home before you go to sleep. There are plenty of things to eat in the fridge, so have something nutritious. Oh," she added, "if you need me, we're downtown, at the Circle View Restaurant. See you later."

Tori couldn't believe her ears. How could her mother brush off the skating dress like that? She'd *promised* she would go over the sketches that night! And hadn't she already spent enough time with Mr. Arnold?

Tori strode into the kitchen and flipped on the light. Then she yanked open the refrigerator door, so hard that a carton of milk in the shelf on the door fell out and spilled on the floor.

"Oh great!" she said. "Who was stupid enough to put the milk there?" Then she remembered that she had done it, when she had left in a rush for practice that morning.

Okay, relax, she told herself as she wiped up the milk with a sponge. Mom will probably start working on my outfit tomorrow. So what if she's been spending time with Roger Arnold lately? They obviously have a lot to discuss about the clothing she's designing for the store. And it's a great boost for Mom's career.

Tori gave a little laugh and started to take out the ingredients for a salad.

But before she had even unwrapped the lettuce, she remembered something her mother had said in her message—that she and Mr. Arnold were having a working dinner at the Circle View Restaurant. Since when was the Circle View Restaurant the place for a business dinner? Were those dramatic views, soft music, and romantic lighting supposed to improve their concentration? What if there was something more than business going on?

Tori swallowed hard and put the salad stuff back. She opened the freezer, pulled out a frozen pizza, and popped it into the oven. Then she went into the living room and plopped down on the cream-colored couch. She flipped on the TV so the big three-story house wouldn't feel so empty and pulled out her homework. She knew her mother didn't want her to do schoolwork in front of the TV, and that she wouldn't approve of pizza for dinner, either, but she didn't care. After all, she thought angrily, why should I be responsible if she's going to drop everything and go out with Mr. Arnold?

When her pizza was ready, she carried it to the living room and sat down on the cream-colored rug. She knew her mother would flip out if she knew Tori was eating in the living room, but too bad. Tonight Tori didn't care. She rushed through her social studies homework between bites of pizza and then tried to work on the problems for math. But she couldn't concentrate very well. She felt tired from practice, and she kept thinking about her mother and Mr. Arnold. Was there something going on between them, or was it all her imagination?

She decided to call Haley. Her friend always had a way of cheering her up.

"Hi, Tori," Haley said when she came on the line. "What's up?"

"Hi. Not much," said Tori. "I'm just hanging out waiting for my mom to come home."

"Your mom's not home yet!" Haley exclaimed. "That's weird!"

"She had to work late with Mr. Arnold," Tori explained. "Over dinner."

"Oh," said Haley.

"Actually," Tori said, trying to sound casual, "they're at the Circle View Restaurant."

"The Circle View," Haley said. "That's pretty fancy. Must be some meeting."

"What do you mean?"

"Well, the Circle View is sort of romantic-like," Haley pointed out.

"I know," Tori admitted glumly. "I was thinking the same thing."

"Wow," said Haley excitedly. "So do you think there's something more going on? Like a date? That'd be pretty cool, huh?"

"I guess." Although Tori didn't really think so at all. "The thing is, my mom and I were supposed to talk about my dress for the competition, and instead she's out with Mr. Arnold," she complained.

"Oh, Tori, what are you worried about?" said Haley. "You must have about a million beautiful outfits you could wear to the competition. Besides, there's nothing wrong with your mom going out on a date."

"Did I say there was?" Tori snapped. With Mrs. Carsen's elegant good looks, she certainly didn't have any problem attracting attention. But she never dated the same guy more than once or twice. Obviously, her mother wasn't interested in getting serious with anyone. Besides, with her busy fashion design business and Tori's skating career to manage, she never had time to spare for anyone else—until now, Tori reminded herself.

"Don't you see, Haley?" Tori complained. "I've been working really hard on this routine with Blake, and I really wanted a new outfit to go with it. If my mom doesn't start making it soon, it's going to be too late."

"Hey, the competition is still two weeks away. Your mom won't let you down," Haley assured her. "We're talking about *your mom*, Skating Mother of the World, right?"

Tori had to laugh when Haley put it like that. "Yeah, I guess you're right. Hey, I should probably be happy to have a little time to myself without her breathing down my neck and telling me what to do every five minutes."

"It's probably kind of cool for her to have a break, too," Haley added. "You know, it must be hard on her, being a single mother. I couldn't imagine my mother doing everything by herself."

"But your mother is different," Tori said. Mrs. Carsen always did everything for Tori. She was always there for her, especially when it came to Tori's skating. Tori didn't expect Haley to understand. Haley's mother was much more laid-back about skating. Once Mrs. Arthur had even suggested Haley skip afternoon practices!

"Hey, listen," Haley said. "If I were you, I'd be happy for your mom. I think it's really amazing that she might have a boyfriend! I'll see you tomorrow morning at the rink, okay?"

"Yeah, okay, Haley. Bye," said Tori.

As she hung up, Tori felt worse than before. Even Haley agreed that her mother's meeting sounded pretty romantic. But Tori knew Haley could never really understand. Tori's family was different. It was just Tori and her mom. Together. A team.

Mrs. Carsen had wanted to be a champion skater herself, which was why she understood Tori's love of skating. It was very important to her mother that Tori get all the encouragement, the support, and the finest training possible. So why wasn't she here tonight working on Tori's dress?

Tori wandered into the entrance hall. She noticed a brightly colored postcard in the pile of mail on the floor under the mail slot. She picked it up. The picture showed snow-covered mountains at sunset. She flipped it over and saw that it was addressed to her; it was from her father.

> *Dear Tori,*
>
> *Hello from Colorado! Had some vacation time, and decided to head out West for some skiing. The mountains are spectacular. Hope all is well with you. Carol sends her best.*
>
> > *Love,*
> > *Dad*

Tori and her father had exchanged a few letters, but she barely knew him. They had met only once— at the Regional competition earlier this year in Lake Placid. She had never met his new wife, Carol, who was, after all, her stepmother. *Stepmother*—the idea seemed kind of funny to Tori. After all, Tori didn't need another mother. She just wanted the one she had to come home. Tori rubbed a muscle in her leg that was sore from practice.

Suddenly she knew exactly how to make herself feel better. A nice, relaxing bubble bath with lilac foaming gel. There was nothing like a hot bath after a long practice.

Ten minutes later she was sudsed up and feeling like a queen in her private kingdom. She piled her shampooed hair high on her head, just the way she'd done when she was a little girl, and pretended to accept the Olympic gold medal on behalf of the United States. Then she settled back into the bubbles and whispered to herself the words her mother had said to her every night since she began skating: "You're a champion, Tori Carsen. A champion to the core."

When she got out of the tub, Tori pulled on her favorite pink-flowered pajamas. She felt much better now. She was no longer mad that her mother was not home yet. As she flopped on her bed with a skating magazine, she assured herself that her mother would start on the skating dress the very next day. And she would probably feel so bad about having left Tori by herself that she would make it the best dress ever!

Tori studied the dresses in the skating magazines for ideas. Tomorrow she'd be able to tell her mother *exactly* what she wanted.

3

Early the next morning, Tori slipped into their silver Jaguar. Her mother sat behind the wheel, sipping from a thermos of coffee. Tori had to be at the rink by five-thirty. Members of Silver Blades practiced every day before and after school. The sun wasn't up yet, so Tori was surprised to see her mom wearing sunglasses.

"Mom, isn't it a little dark out for those?" Tori asked. She couldn't help feeling that her mother was hiding behind the dark glasses.

Tori's mother turned and gazed at her over the top of her sunglasses. She wore a white silk scarf over her blond hair and looked elegant as usual.

"Good morning to you too, Tori." Her mother pushed the glasses onto the top of her head as she drove the Jaguar out of the driveway. "There. Is that better?" Mrs. Carsen asked with a small smile.

Tori didn't smile back. As far as she was concerned her mother had a lot of explaining to do. "Where were you last night?" she asked sharply.

"What do you mean, where was I? Didn't you get my message? Roger and I had to work late. We were downtown. When I came home you were already asleep," Mrs. Carsen explained. "I hope you weren't worried," she added in a concerned tone of voice. "You know you're supposed to listen to the machine, Tori. That's our system, just in case, right?"

"I heard the message," Tori muttered. "So now it's *Roger*, huh? No more Mr. Arnold."

"What?" Her mother sounded distracted. "Oh, yes, well, I'm sure you must realize by now that Roger Arnold and I are becoming good friends, as well as business partners."

Good friends, thought Tori, I wonder what that means. But she decided not to ask. Somehow she wasn't sure she was ready to hear the answer.

"But Tori," her mother went on, "if you heard the message, why are you asking me where I was? You knew I was out with Roger."

"But you said you were going to be home before I fell asleep," Tori said grumpily. "And you weren't, and now you're all tired from being out with *Roger*." Tori made a face as she said the name. "I think it is irresponsible," she added. She was starting to enjoy the chance to criticize her mother for once. See how she likes it, Tori thought.

"What is the problem, Tori?" Mrs. Carsen sounded exasperated. "It's ten after five in the morning, we are in the car, and we are going to be at the rink exactly on time, if not a few minutes early. So what is the big deal?"

So we're going to be on time, thought Tori. That wasn't the point. The point was . . . well, she wasn't exactly sure *what* the point was. But she still didn't think her mother should be getting off that easy.

"Mom, you know you're supposed to be rested in the mornings to take me to practice," she said.

"Tori, please," said her mother. "It's not as if I'm the one who is doing the skating this morning, or any other morning for that matter. You're the skater. I'm only the chauffeur."

Tori couldn't believe her mother just said those words. Only the chauffeur? From any of the other mothers in Silver Blades this might be normal, but coming from Mrs. Carsen, it was absolutely ridiculous. "Mom, are you feeling okay?" Tori asked in amazement.

"I feel great!" Mrs. Carsen answered. "Oh, Tori, it is so wonderful. Seeing my designs featured in Arnold's Department Stores is everything I've worked so hard to accomplish. And Roger really appreciates my talent. It's such a pleasure working with someone who values my efforts."

"What about *me*?" Tori said, a little hurt that she didn't seem to count.

"Of course you appreciate me, I know that, silly. But this is different. Roger is a major businessman, not a little girl. It's completely different," explained Mrs. Carsen.

Tori couldn't believe it. Up until now, she'd always felt she was important to her mother—that they were a team. So now I'm just a little girl, huh? Tori grumbled inwardly. She scrunched down in the leather upholstery and gazed out the window. She decided she was going to ignore her mother as much as possible, difficult as that was with Mrs. Carsen talking so much.

But Mrs. Carsen didn't even seem to notice Tori's bad mood. She babbled on and on about how wonderful Roger was, how funny he was, how sweet he was, how much he wanted to meet Tori. Ugh, Tori thought, how much longer until we get to the rink? I just want this conversation to be over.

"And then Roger came up with an absolutely fabulous idea," Mrs. Carsen went on. "He said he thought we should set aside an entire section of the store to be the Corinne Carsen Boutique, just for my designs. Isn't that marvelous?"

Tori didn't say anything, but again, her mother didn't seem to notice.

"Well, he feels that my clothes are going to be very, very successful. He may even feature them in the window to draw people into the store," Mrs. Carsen continued. "Actually, he's thinking about making Seneca Hills the new headquarters of his company, since he's originally from here. Eventually, though, we might be able to set up Corinne Carsen Boutiques in every Arnold's Department Store across the country. Of course, I would have to work extra hard to make that happen. But still, what an opportunity! Isn't that exciting, Tori?"

Tori glared at her mother. For someone who ought to be tired from having stayed out late the night before, Mrs. Carsen certainly was glowing with excitement. And it was clear that she wasn't getting the message that Tori wasn't interested in talking about Roger Arnold, even if he did help her mother's career. Tori flipped her braid over her shoulder and turned her head away from her mother. She made a face at her reflection in the car window, but her mother didn't see it. Tori started tapping her foot, something that usually annoyed her mother, but Mrs. Carsen didn't seem to notice that, either.

Then, as the rink came into view, she heard her mother say, "Tori? Weren't you listening? I said Roger wants to meet you. I thought tonight would be good. Roger and I will be working again this afternoon, so I'll make arrangements with the Panatis to bring you home from skating. Then the three of us can have dinner together." Mrs. Carsen sighed happily. "I know you're going to *love* Roger, Tori. He's a great guy." As they pulled into a parking space, her mother had a soft smile on her face.

Tori jumped out of the car without a word. She marched over to the rink's big swinging doors, her mother's words still ringing in her ears: "You're going to *love* Roger." Hah! she thought. She hated him already!

4

Tori stormed through the double doors so quickly that they slammed against the wall with a loud bang. Everyone at the rink looked up. Tori shrugged and smiled quickly. The last thing she wanted was for everyone to know how upset she was. "Whoops!" she said lightly, adding a little giggle.

She raced for the locker room, her rose-colored skating bag dangling from her shoulder. Inside, Haley and Danielle were listening to Nikki telling a story. Nikki's eyes were sparkling, and she was smiling.

"Hi, Tori," Haley said.

"Hi, guys," said Tori, still trying to sound cheerful.

"Nikki just told us this really funny story about her mom and dad," said Danielle, laughing a little.

"Listen, Tori, this is the cutest," Haley said. "Go ahead Nikki, tell Tori."

Nikki started right in. "It happened last night after dinner. My dad always makes my mom sit and put her feet up for a while after we eat, and I was in the kitchen doing the dishes. Meanwhile my dad was in the garage sorting out the bottles and cans for the recycling program. We have a couple of those bins for all the different stuff, you know?"

All the girls nodded, and Nikki continued.

"So my mother was watching TV when this story about fishing came on. My dad's really into fishing. Anyway, she wanted him to see it, so she called for him to come quick. Well, he thought it was time for the baby, so he came running in from the garage." She grinned. "But he stepped in one of the bins and got his foot stuck!"

The girls started giggling.

"He came running through the kitchen into the living room with this bin on his foot," said Nikki. "He almost fell over! My mom and I were laughing so hard. It was hysterical."

Nikki, Danielle, and Haley broke out into uncontrollable laughter. Tori managed to laugh along with them. She had to admit, the story *was* pretty funny, but it made her feel a little sad, too. Looking at Nikki and thinking about how happy she and her family were, Tori couldn't help feeling jealous of how cozy and together they all sounded.

"Hey, Tori," Haley said, "how did things go with

your mom and Mr. Arnold last night?" She turned to Nikki and Danielle. "Mrs. Carsen and Mr. Arnold ended up having dinner at the Circle View Restaurant."

"Wow, the Circle View," Danielle said. "Sounds to me like something's going on, Tori."

"It was a *working* dinner," Tori snapped.

"The Circle View sure is a fancy place to have a business meeting, though," Haley teased, still smiling.

"I remember when my family first moved here and we went out to the Circle View for a celebration dinner," Nikki said. "It's so pretty at sunset, the way you can see the lights twinkling in every direction. I guess it must be the most romantic restaurant in Seneca Hills. If you're with the right person," she added.

"And the food is so yummy," Danielle said. "The fettuccine Alfredo's almost as good as my grandmother's."

"What did your mom have? Did she say? I bet she had the lobster," said Haley. "Mmm, all that butter!"

"I have no idea what she ate," Tori said coldly. "I didn't see her until this morning and I didn't ask."

"Why do you sound so mad, Tori?" Danielle asked. "Yesterday I thought you were happy that your mother had this chance to get her designs into Arnold's Department Store. Is something wrong?"

Tori sighed impatiently. "I just don't like it that she was out so late," she admitted. "She was really tired this morning, and she hasn't shown me any of the sketches for my new dress. What if she doesn't get it done in time? I think my dress is more important than some stupid dinner with Mr. Arnold!"

"Oh, right, the dress," Nikki said. "But your mom still has plenty of time to get it done."

"Besides, you have so many dresses, Tori," Haley pointed out.

"Yeah," Danielle said. "You can always wear one of your other dresses. Like that purple one with the white trim, or how about the pink chiffon?"

"But some of the judges have seen it already!" Tori wailed. "I need a *new* dress. A dress that really shows off Blake's choreography. Besides my mom always makes me something new for every competition."

But Tori could see from the looks on their faces that Haley, Nikki, and Danielle didn't have much sympathy for her—probably because none of them had nearly as many skating dresses as she did. Even right now, for practice, they wore T-shirts and leggings with their light blue Silver Blades warm-up jackets. Tori, though, was wearing a beautiful turquoise velvet skating dress with narrow bands of white lace at the throat and wrists, and a matching ribbon at the end of her braid. Tori's mother insisted that Tori dress up, even for practice. Mrs. Carsen said that way Tori would always perform her best, since she would be dressed like a champion.

Tori felt really grumpy now. First there had been the argument with her mom in the car, then Nikki's

cute little family story, and now the dress! If only
Roger Arnold weren't taking up all her mother's time
and attention! Then Tori remembered what her
mother said about how "Roger" was possibly going
to feature Corinne Carsen designs in the window of
the Seneca Hills store to draw people in.

"Mr. Arnold is really only using my mother, and
that's why I'm so upset," Tori lied. "It makes me mad
that there's nothing I can do to help her, and she
doesn't see it."

"What? Why do you say that?" Haley asked with
surprise.

"Well, it's obvious, isn't it? Everyone knows his
business isn't doing well. He needs something, and
he thinks my mom can save this grand opening here
in Seneca Hills," Tori said smugly.

"But Tori, Arnold's Department Stores are all over
the country," Nikki said.

"I mentioned it to Jill last night on the phone, and
she said there is a really big one in Colorado, not too
far from the Ice Academy," Danielle added.

"Sounds like they're doing pretty well to me," said
Haley. "Besides, even if your mom's designs do help
the Seneca Hills store, I doubt that one store can
make all the difference."

"I'm telling you, it's true," Tori insisted, feeling a
little better.

"That's weird," said Danielle. "Because according
to Jill, Arnold's is just about the hottest store in Denver. But you know more about it, I guess."

"Yes, I do," Tori said a little defensively. She just wished everyone would drop the subject.

"Hey, don't look now, but here comes Sarge," Haley said suddenly.

Kathy Bart walked over to the group of friends.

"Good morning, ladies," she said. Kathy coached many of the Silver Blades skaters, including Haley and Nikki. She was in her twenties and wore her dark-blond hair pulled back in a ponytail. "All right, enough talk, let's skate! When I was competing, they didn't have a category for Olympic gossiping."

Sarge was right, Tori thought. Even though Tori's coach was Mr. Weiler, Tori still had a lot of respect for Kathy. Kathy once placed fourth in the Nationals. She had been a top-ranked skater, and now she was a tough coach.

Tori and the others quickly changed into their skates and began their warm-ups. After stretching her hamstrings and practicing a few simple jumps, Tori started powering up to try a triple toe loop. It was a difficult jump for her, and Blake's new routine featured this move twice, so Tori knew she'd better work on it. She often had trouble landing the triple. She had already mastered a double Lutz–double toe loop combination, which she had done in the Regionals at Lake Placid. Winning the bronze had been disappointing for Tori, but she'd been happy to place.

Tori knew she needed to practice her triple toe loop more to gain enough height, but she was sure she could get it. Just as she was about to take off, she noticed Blake watching her from the boards, and it broke her concentration. She completed only one and a half revolutions and almost fell. She was going to have to do a lot better than that.

"Tori!" Mrs. Carsen yelled from the bleachers. "What was that?" Her mother sat near Danielle's mother, but that did not stop her from making her usual comments about Tori's skating.

Tori waved her off. "I know, I know," she answered. "I'm going again." She circled back to gain more speed in her approach. She looked to see if Blake was watching, but he was working with Haley and Patrick now.

Tori tried again, and this time she pulled off a full triple, but it was not nearly high enough. She was going to need a lot more strength to land cleanly on one foot. She glanced over at her mother, expecting the usual criticism, but Mrs. Carsen had her head buried in her small sketchbook. Tori was relieved that her mother hadn't seen the jump. But why wasn't her mother paying attention?

Maybe if I give myself a little more distance, Tori thought, I can get high enough to fit in that third revolution. She skated down the ice toward where Kathy was coaching Martina Nemo. Tori bit her lip and dug in for speed. She had almost completed three revolutions before the ice rushed up. She fell with a thump.

"Tori! Get over here," Mrs. Carsen commanded.

Tori skated over to the side of the rink near where her mother sat in the bleachers.

"Yes, Mom?" She brushed ice shavings off her tights. She always felt a little embarrassed when her mother criticized her in public.

"You're going to have to work harder if you want to get that triple," said Mrs. Carsen.

"I know, I'm trying," Tori sighed.

"I know you are. Just try harder."

"Mom, telling me to try harder is not very helpful. Is that why you called me over here?" Tori huffed.

"No. I wanted to tell you that I'm going to the coffee shop for a little while. I have a lot of details to work out before my meeting with Roger today. Get me when you're done, and I'll drop you off at school. Okay?" Mrs. Carsen said this as though it were the most natural thing in the world for Tori to practice without her supervision.

As Mrs. Carsen collected her briefcase and Tori's school bag and headed for the coffee shop, Tori stared after her, stunned. What's going on? Her mother had never acted this way before.

Tori meandered back to her area of the ice. She did a few figure eights and then glanced up to see if Blake was watching her. He was!

Tori perked up and skated over to him. He looked gorgeous, as usual, with the powder blue of his Silver Blades jacket bringing out the blue of his eyes. When he smiled at Tori, she stopped worrying about her mother and smiled back.

"Hey there, champ," Blake said teasingly. "Looks like you're having some difficulty with that triple toe loop."

Tori blushed a little. She hadn't realized Blake was watching her practice.

"I can't seem to get enough height," she admitted, tracing circles in the ice with the toe of her blade. "Have any suggestions?" she asked with a smile.

"I've got to run through this routine again with Haley and Patrick," Blake said. "And practice is almost over. But we'll get to it this afternoon, okay?" He gave her shoulder a pat and then skated over to his waiting pairs team.

Tori circled back with a sigh. She thought of trying the jump again, but decided to put it off. After all, why should she care if no one else did? She'd try the toe loop again at the afternoon session. She half-heartedly did some more figure eights and a few waltz jumps and scanned the rink to see who she could chat with. If her mother was going to spend the practice drinking coffee, why should she knock herself out?

What was her mother thinking about, anyway? Obviously not about Tori, the triple toe loop, or the dress she had promised to make. Tori sighed deeply. No, she was thinking about Roger Arnold and his stupid stores.

"Watch out!" she heard someone cry.

Tori looked up and nearly crashed into Danielle. She had been so lost in thought that she hadn't even seen Danielle coming straight at her until it was almost too late.

"Oh, sorry, Dani," Tori said.

"Wow, that was close," said Danielle breathlessly. "I was coming out of my double axel, and you almost skated right into me. We both could have been seriously hurt."

Tori knew that each skater was supposed to watch out for others practicing their jumps. An injury could keep a skater out for weeks—or forever. Just look at what had happened to Jill.

"I know." Tori was annoyed with herself now. "I said I was sorry. I guess I was thinking about why I'm having such a hard time with my triple toe loop."

"I saw," Danielle replied. "Did you try bending your knee more to get more height?"

"Yes, of course I did," Tori shot back. She didn't mean to be rude, but her anger at her mom made her snap at her friend.

"Well, listen, I'll talk to you later," said Danielle. "Mr. Weiler's waiting for me. Got to go!" She skated off.

Tori gazed around. Everybody else was busy working on their routines. She knew she should be more serious, too, but she couldn't seem to concentrate. She checked the wall clock. Ten minutes left to practice. Well, maybe she'd change out of her skating stuff a little early this time. After all, it wasn't as if anyone would notice.

In the locker room, as she changed into her

cream-colored turtleneck and plaid pleated mini-skirt, Tori thought again about how strange it felt to be on the ice without her mother watching. And as she pictured her mother sitting in the coffee shop thinking about Roger Arnold—unaware that her daughter sneaked out of practice early—Tori felt downright miserable. So much for the Carsen team, she thought with a sigh.

5

Later that afternoon, back at the rink before practice, Tori sat on a bench in the locker room and fumbled with the laces of her skates. For what seemed like the hundredth time that day, she thought about how much she didn't want to meet Roger Arnold at dinner. She was definitely not looking forward to going home after practice, and wished there were some way to get out of her mother's plans. Tori didn't see why it was so important for her to meet the great Roger, anyway. After all, Mr. Arnold and her mother would probably only talk about the stores and other boring stuff.

Danielle and Haley sat down on the bench near Tori and began lacing their skates, too. They were talking about one of their favorite topics: food. It was especially difficult for Danielle to watch her weight.

Haley, however, never had any problem with hers, which was a good thing, because she loved to eat.

"Mmm, I can't wait until practice is over," Haley said. "My mom has her art class over at Seneca College tonight, and that means that Dad and Morgan and I get to order a mushroom pizza, my favorite."

"I can't wait, either," Danielle said. "We're having manicotti tonight, and I've been starving myself all day just so I can eat as much as I want."

Haley looked at her sternly. "How can you practice if you don't keep up your strength, Dani? Starving all day is not a good idea."

"I know, I know," said Danielle. "Starving might be too strong a word." She checked her laces. "Let's just say that I was so sensible that it *felt* like starving."

Haley laughed, then looked over at Tori. "What are you and your mom doing for dinner?"

Tori shrugged and straightened her tights. "I'm not really sure," she lied. After the way her friends had talked about Roger Arnold and her mother, she wasn't about to bring up the subject again.

"Oh, Tori," Danielle said warmly, "why don't you have dinner with us? You've never had such good manicotti in your life, I promise. Since my mother's driving you anyway, you could just come home with us. Want to?"

Tori hesitated for a minute. It was true that she really didn't want to go home, but her mother *was* expecting her to meet Mr. Arnold.

"I'd really like to, Dani," she began, "but I don't know . . ."

"I'm sure it'll be no problem," Danielle said. "Grandma always makes tons. Maybe you could call your mom and ask her."

There was nothing Tori wanted more than to go to Danielle's for dinner, but she knew her mother would never agree to let her miss meeting Mr. Arnold. "I don't think so, Dani," she said with a sigh. "But thanks anyway."

Tori hoped that skating would take her mind off things, but after a few minutes of warming up out on the ice, she still couldn't stop thinking about her mother and Mr. Arnold. Her concentration was even worse than it had been that morning. Maybe it was because she felt so alone without her mother's voice guiding her through her practice. And to make matters worse, everyone seemed to notice her mother's absence.

While Tori prepared to work on some toe loops, Mr. Weiler skated over and asked, "Tori, is your mother ill?"

"No, she's not, Mr. Weiler," Tori answered her coach.

"It's just that it's so unusual for her to be absent," he said. "Is everything okay?"

"Oh, everything's fine," Tori replied with a fake smile. She certainly didn't want Mr. Weiler to know that her mother was spending all her time with

Roger Arnold. "She's got a big project she's working on," she added.

"Oh, I see," said Mr. Weiler. "Well, back to practice. See you later."

As he skated off, Kathy Bart whizzed up, stopping with a scratch spin. "I meant to ask you this morning, is your mom okay?" the coach asked. "She left early, and now I see she's not here. Is there anything wrong?"

Kathy doesn't even coach me, Tori thought, and she's noticed that my mom's not where she should be. No wonder I can't get any work done, with everybody bothering me about my mother like this! But she stopped herself before she snapped. She knew Kathy meant well.

"Thanks for asking," Tori managed to say. "She has a lot of work to do for a big project. She'll be here tomorrow." I hope, she added to herself.

"Okay, well, I'm glad to hear that everything's fine," Kathy said and skated off without a backward glance.

Yeah, just fine, Tori thought. Then she noticed Blake staring at her from the other side of the rink. She knew she should work on her triple toe loop. He was probably ready to help her nail it, as he'd said that morning. She had to get that jump down, she just had to. But right now she wasn't feeling very sure of herself. She decided to start with something easier and then work her way up to trying the triple.

After all, the competition was still almost two weeks away.

Finally, after dawdling for nearly twenty minutes, she decided to give the jump a go. But every time she tried it, she only managed two and a half revolutions. She wasn't getting enough speed up to reach the height she needed.

As she came to a standstill after her last try, she turned to find Blake watching her.

"You can do a lot better than that, Tori," he said sternly.

Tori hung her head and then looked up at Blake from beneath a few stray curls. Hearing Blake criticize her was no fun, even though compared to her mother's comments it was nothing. But she could tell he was serious. "You're right, Blake. I'm just not concentrating very well today," she admitted, shrugging her shoulders.

"Well, maybe you should try focusing a little more," he suggested. "I put in a lot of effort to create a challenging and good-looking routine for you. I hope you won't let me down."

Tori chewed her lower lip and didn't say anything.

Blake softened a bit. "Look, I understand if you're having an off day, Tori. It happens to the best of us."

"I'll do better tomorrow, I promise," Tori said sincerely.

But deep inside she was not really sure about that. *If only my mother was here I wouldn't be having this* problem, she thought resentfully. Now I might not have the triple toe loop down by Rochester, and it will all be Roger Arnold's fault!

"All right," Blake said. "But you're not getting off so easy today." He grinned. "Let's see your routine from the top."

Tori ran through the first half of her routine, but when she came to the triple toe loop, she fell.

When she finished her program, she could tell from the look on Blake's face how poorly she'd performed. "That's enough for today," he said. "You may need to get in some extra practice between now and the competition, though. Maybe we can put time in together over the weekend. I'll see what I can do with my schedule."

As Blake's words sank in, Tori suddenly got an idea—one that would get her out of meeting Roger Arnold!

Tori skated off the ice happily. Even though she was sorry that she had disappointed Blake, she was sure she could make it up to him by the competition. In the meantime, she had to take care of something.

She hurried to the phone booth and carefully thought out the message she would leave for her mother. She knew Mrs. Carsen wouldn't be home yet, so there was no chance of having to explain herself to her mom directly. She dropped in a quarter, dialed the number, and cleared her throat. The machine came on.

"Hi, Mom. It's me. I'm calling to let you know that

Blake wants to work with me some more on my routine, so that he can be sure that I get it down in time for Rochester. He worked really hard on the choreography for me, and you know how special that is. He went out to do something, but he'll be back at the rink in a while, so we'll be skating late tonight."

Tori wanted her mother to know that she wasn't the only one who was busy. Even if Mrs. Carsen was too busy for Tori's skating, there were other people who were not.

"And Dani is staying late for practice also, so we're going to grab something to eat before, and then I can drive home with the Panatis so I won't have to interrupt your dinner date," Tori continued. "I'm sorry to miss it, but we'll probably be pretty late. You know how important the competition is to all of us. Talk to you later. Bye!"

Tori hung up the phone with a slam. That would teach her mother to try and make her meet Roger Arnold.

Tori spotted Danielle heading toward the locker room.

"Oh, Dani, Dani!" she called happily, running up to her. "Guess what? It turns out that my mom's working late, so I can come to dinner after all!"

"That's great, Tori." Danielle grinned.

It sure is, thought Tori, feeling a lot better now that she had outsmarted her mother. After all, she reminded herself as she followed Danielle into the locker room, her mother seemed to be doing whatever she wanted these days, so why shouldn't Tori?

6

"So, Tori," said Mr. Panati for the third or fourth time that evening, "I'll be happy to give you a ride home anytime you're ready."

"Uh, okay, Mr. Panati, thanks," Tori said quickly.

Dinner was long over at the Panatis', and Tori's main problem now was how to stay away from home for as long as possible. She wanted to be absolutely sure that Mr. Arnold was gone first, so she kept finding excuses to stay at Danielle's.

First, after dinner, she'd offered to clean up the kitchen with Danielle, and then, after the last dish had been dried and put away, Tori had suggested a family tournament of checkers. The surprise winner was Grandma Panati.

"Hey, how about a rematch, Grandma Panati?"

Tori suggested now. "I'm sure I can beat you this time."

"Tori, you are a fine player for your age, but I am not so young anymore," Grandma Panati said. "It's time for this old lady to call it a night."

"Are you sure?" Tori asked hopefully. "Or, don't you want to tell me again how you won against Grandpa Panati back in Italy?"

"Oh no," groaned Nicholas. "Not that story again!"

"That was such a long time ago," said Grandma Panati, waving a hand in the air. "We used to play checkers all the time, and he always won. He used to say that the girl who could beat him at checkers was the girl he wanted to marry."

"And you knew he was the one for you," Danielle chimed in.

"Oh, yes," Grandma Panati said. "He was very handsome, and I loved how kind and considerate he was. So I practiced and practiced checkers with my own grandfather. And one day I won. But I have always wondered," she added with a smile, "if Dani and Nicholas's grandfather let me win. I was very pretty back then, and as you know I make a very special sauce." She laughed and patted Tori's hand as she stood up.

"Good night, Mother," Mr. Panati said, glancing at the clock again. It was almost nine o'clock, later than usual for the members of Silver Blades to be up. "Tori, I really do think it's time I drive you home. You girls still have to get up early, unless you've decided to give up skating and become a checkers champion instead."

Tori laughed, but nodded after seeing Danielle yawn and rubbing her eyes.

"I have to admit I'm getting really sleepy myself," Danielle said. "This was fun, though, Tori. I'm so glad you came over."

"Thank you for having me, everybody. I had a lot of fun," Tori replied.

"Are you sure you don't want me to call your mother?" asked Mrs. Panati. "Maybe I should let her know you're on your way."

"Oh no, Mrs. Panati, but thank you," Tori said quickly. "I left a message for her already. That's our system."

Mr. Panati stood at the door while Tori collected her skating bag and zipped up her jacket. She gazed around for a minute, looking for another way to put off her trip home. But all she saw was Danielle yawning again.

"Okay, then, good night," Tori said, waving to Nicholas and Danielle.

They waved back as she and Mr. Panati walked to the car. Seeing the light coming from the open door and the Panati family looking out, Tori felt a little sad. She wished things would get back to normal between her and her mom.

In the car, Mr. Panati did not say much, which was fine with Tori. She was lost in her own thoughts. Mostly she was happy that the evening had been so much fun and that her plan for avoiding Mr. Arnold had worked out so well. Maybe she'd never have to meet him at all.

Mr. Panati pulled up to Tori's driveway. Lights shone in every window, and the house looked welcoming.

"I'd take you to your front door, but there doesn't seem to be room in the driveway," Mr. Panati said, peering through the windshield at Mrs. Carsen's silver Jaguar and another car Tori didn't recognize. "Is this okay?"

"Just great," Tori replied with an edge in her voice as she stared at the strange car. "I mean, thank you very much for driving me home, Mr. Panati. I really appreciate it."

She collected her things and waved as Mr. Panati drove off. As she slowly walked up the driveway, around the strange, black, expensive-looking car, a feeling of dread came over her. It was Roger Arnold's car, she just knew. But what was he doing here so late?

She opened the front door very quietly and stepped inside. She heard her mother's voice and a man's in the kitchen, laughing. Maybe she could just sneak up to her room and hide under the covers and they wouldn't notice. But the front door closed behind her with a bang, and Tori flinched.

"Tori?" her mother called out from the kitchen. "Is that you?"

"Yes." For once, Tori was sorry she hadn't listened

to her mother's nagging about not letting the front door slam behind her.

"Come on in, sweetie, I want you to meet someone," her mother said.

Tori straightened her shoulders, took a deep breath, and started toward the kitchen.

Her mother and Mr. Arnold stood behind the big kitchen counter, drying dishes together. Tori was surprised at how flushed and happy her mother looked, but forgot about it as soon as Mr. Arnold turned around to meet her.

Tori glanced at Mr. Arnold long enough to see that he was tall, with dark hair and brown eyes. But as soon as his eyes met hers, she turned away and ignored him. Opening the refrigerator and pouring a glass of milk, she tried her best to pretend that neither her mother nor Mr. Arnold was there. When she looked up, she could see that her mother was embarrassed, but Tori didn't care. She just gulped the milk down faster.

"Tori," said Mrs. Carsen, "I'd like you to meet Mr. Arnold."

"I've really been looking forward to this moment, Tori," Mr. Arnold said, offering his hand.

Tori gazed coldly at it and slowly put down her glass to shake hands. "How do you do," she said primly. She walked over to the sink and began rinsing out her glass.

"How was practice, sweetie?" Mrs. Carsen asked. Tori could tell her mother was trying to smooth over the awkward moment. "You look a little tired. Did Blake give you a good workout?"

"It was fine," Tori lied. "But if you'll excuse me, I have to go to bed now. I'm kind of tired." Tori started toward the kitchen door, but Mrs. Carsen stopped her.

"Tori, please wait just a few minutes. We were so disappointed that you had to miss dinner," Mrs. Carsen said. "Mr. Arnold stayed especially to meet you."

Tori sighed loudly.

Her mother gave her a sharp look, but then smiled at Mr. Arnold. "Why don't we all sit down in the living room?" Mrs. Carsen suggested brightly. "And you can tell Mr. Arnold about the routine you're working on for the Rochester competition."

Silently Tori trudged into the living room. Maybe her mother could force her to sit with Roger Arnold, but she couldn't make Tori like him.

They all sat down in the living room—Mr. Arnold on one of the plushly upholstered cream-colored chairs, Mrs. Carsen on the edge of an antique wooden chair, and Tori on the corner of the couch that was farthest away from Mr. Arnold.

"So," Mr. Arnold said to Tori with a smile, "your mom tells me that you are a very dedicated and talented skater. It sounds like a lot of hard work."

"Yes, it is," Tori answered. She stared down at her hands folded in her lap and suddenly realized that she really *was* very tired. She stifled a yawn.

"Oh, you poor thing," Mrs. Carsen said with concern. "Go ahead and go to bed. I'll be up to say good night soon."

"Yes, well, champions have to get their rest," said Mr. Arnold quietly. He regarded Tori closely. "You look so much like your mom. Such beautiful women in this family," he said, gazing at Mrs. Carsen.

"Why thank you, Roger," Tori's mother said cheerfully. She turned to Tori. "Tori, guess what? To make up for tonight, Roger's going to take us out to the Circle View Restaurant tomorrow night for a special dinner. Won't that be nice?" she chirped.

Yeah, really nice, thought Tori. She was about to make up some excuse for not going when her mother caught her eye. Tori could see from the expression on her mother's face that there was no way she was going to get out of it.

"Okay, fine, Mom," Tori replied with a sigh. "I'm going to bed now. Good night."

"Good night, Tori," called Mr. Arnold after her. "See you tomorrow night."

"Yeah, unfortunately," Tori mumbled to herself as she left the room.

7

After practice the next afternoon, Tori was slipping on her skate guards in the bleachers when she saw her mother and Mr. Arnold enter the rink. They were supposed to pick her up for dinner, but not for another half hour. Why were they here so early?

Tori watched them head toward the admission booth, where tickets were sold for the public skating session. What were they doing? Tori gasped. Her mother *couldn't* be thinking of skating in the public session, could she? Her mother hadn't skated in years. And why would she want to skate at a public session? The rink was always too crowded with people who couldn't skate, falling down and crashing into each other.

Haley strolled over to Tori and dropped her skate bag and schoolbooks on the bench. "Hey, is that Mr.

Arnold with your mom over there?" she asked excitedly. "Not bad! He's pretty good-looking," she said approvingly.

"I guess," Tori said sulkily.

"Tall, dark, and handsome is hard to beat." Haley grinned at Tori. "What's the matter?"

What's the matter? Tori almost shouted. Only that her mom and Mr. Arnold were actually coming right up to them and sitting down!

"Hi, Mrs. Carsen," Haley said. "I haven't seen you at practice much lately. I hear you're pretty busy these days." Haley's green eyes danced mischievously.

"I have been working a lot recently," Mrs. Carsen admitted, then turned to Tori. "Dear, aren't you going to introduce your friend to Mr. Arnold?"

"Haley, this is Mr. Arnold," Tori said flatly.

"You know Arnold's Department Stores, of course, Haley," Mrs. Carsen added.

"Nice to meet you." Haley extended her hand.

"The pleasure is all mine, Haley," Mr. Arnold said as they shook hands heartily.

"Tori," said Mrs. Carsen, "before we go to the Circle View, I thought it would be fun for all of us to skate a little. Haley, would you like to join us?"

"Oh, no, Mrs. Carsen," Haley answered quickly. "Thanks anyway, but I'm catching a ride home with Kathy, and I see she's waiting for me over there. Got to go! Bye. Nice to meet you, Mr. Arnold."

"See ya, Haley," Tori said, but her friend was already gone. I don't blame her for running away, thought Tori. Skating at the evening session! What an embarrassing idea. None of the members of the skating club *ever* skated at the public sessions. It was considered totally uncool. Especially with two grown-ups! Tori couldn't believe her mother had suggested that they go skating with Mr. Arnold. He probably can't skate at all, she thought.

"Let's go get you some skates, Roger. Coming, Tori?" Mrs. Carsen raised her eyebrows expectantly.

Tori shook her head. "I'll wait for you here," she said. The idea of going up to the rental desk with Mr. Arnold and her mother horrified her. As she waited, Tori thought grimly, This is going to be the most humiliating experience of my entire life.

She hoped no one she knew was still at the rink. Fidgeting, she scanned the ice arena. With its two Olympic-size rinks and its stark white interior, the Seneca Hills Ice Arena was pretty impressive.

Tori watched as Mack, the sweet old guy who drove the Zamboni, cleaned the ice for the public session. She always loved seeing the ice become like new again. As Mack drove past the waiting crowd, he waved to Tori. She waved back, knowing that everybody was going to see her now for sure.

But there is no way I'm going out on the ice, Tori thought, climbing up a few rows in the bleachers.

She bent over and loosened her laces. Draping her light blue Silver Blades warm-up jacket over her knees, she leaned back and watched the crowd move onto the ice. She spotted Mr. Arnold and her mother among the skaters. Tori noticed right away that her mother was the only decent skater out there.

Mr. Arnold was clearly not at home on the ice. He clutched the barrier, trying to keep his feet from slipping out from under him. In another minute he would fall—Tori was certain of it. That'll teach him, she thought.

But Mrs. Carsen took his hand, and after a few more turns around the rink, Mr. Arnold was able to leave the barrier and move with the crowd. Tori watched as her mother skated by his side. Every time Mr. Arnold was about to fall, Mrs. Carsen held his arm. The two of them laughed and smiled and did not seem to notice that Tori wasn't on the ice. Why am I even here? she thought. Not that I *want* to be included in their stupid skating lesson, but at least they could have the courtesy to notice that I'm not with them.

After a few more turns around the rink, Mr. Arnold stopped to lean over with his hands on his knees and take a few deep breaths. Then he and Mrs. Carsen skated to a group of benches. Mr. Arnold plopped down, and Mrs. Carsen headed up the bleachers to Tori, a big smile on her face. Tori noticed that she looked relaxed and very pretty, with a flush on her cheeks.

"Hey, Mom, you should skate more often. You look great out there," Tori said as her mother sat down next to her.

"Why, thank you, Tori," Mrs. Carsen replied. "That's the nicest thing you've said to me in days."

Tori stared down at her skates. It was true, things hadn't been very good between her and her mother for the last week or so. But that's Roger Arnold's fault, not mine, Tori reminded herself.

"I really wish you would make the effort to be pleasant to Roger," her mother continued. "You can be so charming when you want to be." She tucked a stray curl of hair behind Tori's ear. "Please, I'm asking you for me, just try a little."

"I *am* trying," Tori lied. Why was it so important to her mother that she and Roger Arnold get along, anyway? Then Tori thought of something. "Hey, Mom," she said, "can I ask *you* something?"

"Of course. You can always ask me anything. What is it?" Mrs. Carsen asked.

"Well, what about my dress?" Tori began. "I can't believe that you haven't shown me any sketches or anything. The competition is in less than two weeks. What if you can't get it done in time?"

"Tori, you know that getting my designs into Roger's store is a major opportunity for me," Mrs. Carsen explained. "Couldn't you just be a little understanding about this one dress?"

"Well, I guess," Tori replied. "But are you still going to make it?"

Her mother sighed. "Frankly, Tori," she said, "your dress is not top priority right now. But I'll do my best."

Tori couldn't believe her ears. *Do her best,* what was that supposed to mean? Was her mom trying to tell her that she might not make her dress after all? After she had promised? Tori was furious. Couldn't her mother understand how important it was to her to have a new dress to go with her new routine for Rochester? Tori could feel her cheeks getting hot.

"M-Mom," she sputtered, "you *told* me you were going to make me a dress for Rochester! I can't believe this. It's all because of that stupid Roger Arnold!"

"Tori! That's quite enough! Lower your voice this instant," Mrs. Carsen hissed. "I don't know who you think you are, young lady, but I am very disappointed in you."

Tori turned away and saw Mr. Arnold clunking up the bleachers toward them in his rental skates.

"Now, listen to me, Tori," Mrs. Carsen continued in a low but stern voice. "We are going to skate, all three of us, and you *will* be polite and well behaved. And that is final. We can talk about your dress later."

Tori had to blink back tears as Mr. Arnold sat down on the bench. She watched as her mother gave him a big smile and patted his arm.

"Okay," he said. "I'm ready to try again. What do you say, Tori, will you show me some of those championship moves of yours?" He turned to Mrs. Carsen and joked, "I think I'm ready to try a flying squirrel, or whatever it's called."

"Camel," Tori corrected sharply, relacing her skates as slowly as possible.

Mrs. Carsen eyed her warningly.

"It's called a flying camel," Tori added with slightly less chill in her voice.

"I'd love to see you do one, Tori," Mr. Arnold prompted, smiling at Mrs. Carsen.

"Then we better get on the ice," Mrs. Carsen said. "Let's go, Tori."

The three of them skated around the rink a few times and then glided to the center of the ice. Tori demonstrated a flying camel and a few waltz jumps and circled her mother and Mr. Arnold with a series of backward crossovers before landing a double sal-chow and stopping with a scratch spin. She had attracted a small crowd, and Mr. Arnold led the group in applause. Then Tori skated over to her mother.

"I hope you're happy now," she said coldly. "I can feel a cramp coming on, so I'm going to rest, if you don't mind."

Normally her mother would be totally alarmed about a cramp and would insist on helping Tori massage it out. But now she only nodded absentmindedly, and turned to Mr. Arnold—as if she didn't even care!

Blinking back tears, Tori left the ice, ran to the locker room, and changed.

By the time she returned, it looked as if Mr. Arnold had had enough. He sat on a bench, rubbing his feet as he changed back into his shoes.

"I'm starved, and there's a lobster calling my name," he joked. "Are the two most beautiful and talented ladies in all of Seneca Hills ready to accept my invitation to dinner?"

"Roger, you are so sweet," said Mrs. Carsen, taking the arm he offered her. "Okay, let's go!"

Tori had to admit, dinner at the Circle View Restaurant was a treat as always. Mr. Arnold ordered lobster, and Tori and her mother had grilled shrimp. With its soft lighting, peach-colored tablecloths, and beautiful white flower centerpieces on every table, the Circle View was definitely the nicest restaurant in Seneca Hills. And the view out of the enormous plate glass windows was beautiful, Tori thought. Too bad she had to share it, *and her mom,* with Mr. Arnold.

Mr. Arnold was very talkative. Tori could tell he was really trying to win her over. But she could also tell he was doing it to impress her mother. Too bad it's not going to work, she thought smugly.

As the waiter cleared his empty plate, Mr. Arnold said, "That skating really gave me an appetite. I knew it would be difficult, but I didn't expect it to be so exhausting. You must be quite an athlete, Tori. I play a lot of tennis myself. I have been a tennis nut ever since I was your age. I'm hoping to get your mom out on the courts and show her a thing or two. At least in tennis you get to keep your feet on solid ground."

Mrs. Carsen smiled appreciatively. "I'd love to learn to play, Roger. It sounds like fun. Doesn't it, Tori?" She looked at Tori expectantly.

Tori's mouth was full, so she just nodded and then stared down at her still full plate. Since Mr. Arnold was talking so much, she didn't think she really needed to add anything. But she saw her mother purse her lips disapprovingly. Tori swallowed. "Sure."

"It's always nice to have a regular partner. It really helps to improve your game," Mr. Arnold continued. "That's probably similar to your skating club, right? It makes a difference if you're part of a team."

A team, Tori thought glumly, that's what *we* used to be—Mom and me. Until *you* came along. It seemed obvious to her that Mr. Arnold was trying to break up the Carsen team. She felt a tear start to form and quickly stared into her plate again, so that Mr. Arnold couldn't see how upset she was.

"You know," Roger Arnold continued, "I was married once, but it didn't last very long. I always thought that if my ex-wife had played tennis with me, it might have been different."

Mrs. Carsen smiled at Tori. "Tori and I think of ourselves as a team," she said. "I know it makes a big difference in our family." She reached across the table for Tori's hand.

Ignoring her mother's hand, Tori pushed her chair back from the table.

"Excuse me, please," she managed to say without letting her voice tremble too much. "I have to use the ladies' room."

Inside the rest room, she splashed some water on her face and looked in the mirror. There, that felt better. But why couldn't her mother see how Mr. Arnold was coming between them?

After taking a deep breath, she felt ready to return to the table and finish her meal.

"Tori, I hope you are as proud of your mother as she is of you," Mr. Arnold said when she sat down again. "Her designs are the freshest I've seen in a long time. I think the Corinne Carsen Boutiques are going to be the shining star of Arnold's Department Stores."

"Oh, Roger," said Tori's mother. "Thank you."

Oh, Roger, Tori repeated to herself. Give me a break. Even my own friends don't sound so goofy around boys.

The waiter came to take their order for dessert. Tori ordered chocolate mousse, her favorite.

"I don't know if your mother mentioned it to you," Mr. Arnold went on, "but I'm featuring her designs in the windows of the Seneca Hills store for the grand opening. We're having a big sales promotion that day—I've ordered special banners and balloons. And everything in the store will be half price! That, together with your mom's designs, will bring the customers in for sure."

Tori rolled her eyes a little and glanced at her mother, but Mrs. Carsen frowned and shook her head slightly. Tori sighed. She thought the half-price sale sounded really tacky, and she knew her mother would, too, if she'd just stop mooning over Mr. Arnold.

"In fact, I'm thinking of opening up Corinne Carsen Boutiques in all the Arnold's Department Stores," he went on. "I'm also thinking of taking your mother on a trip to visit the Montreal store soon. Montreal is a terrific town, and I know a lovely little inn there. We could make a weekend of it. And I'd like you to come, too, Tori. We could get to know each other better. It would be fun."

"I have to practice, Mr. Arnold," Tori said. "There's no way I could go."

Her mother shot her another warning look.

"But thanks for the offer," Tori added lamely.

"That's okay, Tori. I admire your dedication," Roger Arnold said heartily. "Anyway, traveling isn't everything it's cracked up to be. I know I'm tired of it. With all the stores we have across the country, it seems like I'm never home."

He looked deeply into Mrs. Carsen's eyes. Her mother gazed right back, blushing.

Oh, puh-lease, Tori thought, this is too much!

"I've always dreamed of settling down in my hometown," Mr. Arnold said softly. "I'm thinking about coming back to Seneca Hills for good now."

Settling down. Tori thought wildly, what was *that* supposed to mean?

And now Mr. Arnold was holding her mother's hand. Suddenly it was all too clear to Tori. Roger Arnold wanted to *marry* her mother! Mrs. Carsen might become the new Mrs. Arnold! In her most terrifying nightmares, Tori had never imagined anything worse.

8

The next morning Tori glanced across the car seat at her mother for the third time. They were on their way to the rink. Mrs. Carsen had not said a single word to her daughter for the entire ride. Tori could tell her mother was furious with her.

Then, as they pulled into a parking space at Seneca Hills Ice Arena, her mother just about exploded. "Tori, I absolutely cannot get over your behavior toward Roger last night."

Tori slouched down in the seat as she waited for her mother to finish.

"Under *any* circumstances, I would have been embarrassed by your little performance at dinner," Mrs. Carsen continued. "But to do that to me with Roger, who you *know* is very important to me, both professionally and personally, well, it was too much."

"Mom, I don't know what you're talking about," Tori protested lamely. "I didn't do anything."

"That's exactly what I'm talking about!" her mother snapped back. "You barely said a word, you hardly looked at either one of us, and all this after I specifically asked you to make a special effort."

"*He* was doing all the talking," Tori said, pouting. "I couldn't have gotten a word in if I tried."

"But you *didn't* try! You didn't try at all!" said her mother. "I was particularly embarrassed and hurt when you suddenly left the table like that. It was so rude, Tori, really. You know Roger is very important to me."

Tori was silent. What about *me*, she thought, fighting back tears. Aren't *I* important to you anymore?

As if she were reading Tori's mind, Mrs. Carsen added, "You only think about yourself."

They sat in silence for a moment, and then Tori reached to open the car door. If her mother thought she was so self-centered, there was no point in saying anything more. Besides, she was afraid that if she did, she would burst out crying. She couldn't believe this was happening. Roger Arnold was coming between her and her mother—and her mother couldn't even see it!

They walked toward the rink without exchanging another word. Tori was miserable. Why couldn't things go back to the way they were. She even wished her mother would go back to yelling at her about her skating. But her mother didn't seem to care about that anymore—now that Roger Arnold was in the picture.

Fine, Tori thought, as she pushed ahead of her mother into the locker room. If she's not going to worry about my skating anymore, then neither will I. I'll just do whatever I want, and then we'll see if she's really stopped paying attention. In the back of her mind, Tori was sure her mother would come to her senses when she saw how Tori's skating was suffering.

After changing into her mint green, V-neck skating dress, Tori stretched her muscles by the edge of the rink for what seemed a long time. She glared at her mother in the bleachers, but Mrs. Carsen's head was buried in her sketchbook again and she didn't seem to notice that Tori wasn't even on the ice yet. Finally, after receiving a few inquisitive looks from a couple of the other skaters and coaches, Tori realized she'd better get out there.

She skated to the center of the ice and practiced some easy spins, purposely not doing a particularly good job of them. After finishing a really bad one, she sneaked a peek at her mother.

But Mrs. Carsen was leaning over her sketchbook. When she finally did look up, it was to wave a quick hello to Mr. Weiler as he walked toward his office. Then she went back to her work.

Tori couldn't believe it. Her mother wasn't paying attention to her at all! She leaned against the barrier and watched some of the other Silver

Blades skaters practice their routines. It seemed to Tori that everybody was only concerned with themselves and no one had any time for her, not even the coaches.

Blake was working with Haley and Patrick on their pairs routine again. It was starting to look really good, Tori thought.

Danielle was working on her double axel. That was a really advanced jump for her, but Mr. Weiler obviously thought Dani could do it. It had taken Jill Wong quite some time to land her first double axel, even practicing six hours a day at the International Ice Academy in Denver with two of the best coaches in the country, Ludmila Petrova and Simon Wells. Danielle definitely had her work cut out for her, but she was trying, which was a lot more than Tori could say about herself.

Tori sighed. The Rochester competition was only nine days away, and she had made little progress with her triple toe loop. She should work on it now—even if her mother didn't seem to care what she was doing.

Tori made a few attempts at improving her jump, but only landed shakily on two feet, and that about half the time. She looked up at her mother again, but Mrs. Carsen was oblivious, buried in her work. It seemed everybody was concentrating today except Tori. She decided to review the easier parts of her routine, and soon practice was over.

Tori hurried to the locker room to change, and was

surprised to see Danielle and Haley already there, waiting for her.

"Hey, Tori," said Danielle in a low voice, "can we talk to you a sec?"

"Sure." Tori shrugged out of her skating dress. "What's up?"

"It's about a present for Nikki," said Danielle.

"For Nikki?" Tori asked, bewildered.

"For the baby, silly," Haley told her.

"For Nikki's mother," Danielle explained.

"Oh, yeah. Sure," Tori said, but she was too concerned about her own mother to think about anyone else's right now.

"You have to help us think of something really good," Danielle said. "Jill wants to chip in, too."

"We want it to be something nice, but we aren't going to have a lot of money to spend," said Haley.

"Yeah, okay, great," said Tori. "Whatever." She dressed quickly. She didn't feel like talking about Nikki's perfect family.

"That's the problem," said Danielle. "We're stuck about what to get. But you're really good with stuff like that, Tori. We thought maybe you could come up with an idea."

"Fine," said Tori, a little impatiently.

Luckily, at that moment Nikki came toward them. Haley nudged Tori to keep quiet.

"Hey guys, what's up?" asked Nikki.

"Um, nothing," Danielle answered, looking a little nervous.

"Okay, well, see you this afternoon," said Haley.

"Yeah, see you then," echoed Danielle. She shot Tori a meaningful glance, but Tori ignored her. Tori had more important things on her mind.

Later that day, Mrs. Carsen had to meet with a fabric designer, so the Panatis drove Tori home from the afternoon practice. As she pushed through the side door into the empty house, Tori was actually glad that her mom wasn't there. She sure wasn't looking forward to seeing her. Her mother had seemed so angry that morning. Too angry, Tori thought, throwing down her bag. After all, it was just a stupid dinner. Besides, Tori was the one who should be angry. *She* was the one who'd been promised a skating dress!

Tori checked the answering machine, but there were no messages. Then she saw her name on an envelope in the pile of mail underneath the slot in the front door. A letter for her! She picked it up and recognized her father's handwriting.

Well, at least someone's thinking about me, Tori thought as she raced upstairs. She threw herself on the yellow-and-white checkered bedspread and quickly ripped open the envelope.

Dear Tori,

Well, Carol and I are back from Col-orado. It's Sunday morning here in Lake Placid, and it's starting to warm up a little bit. We took a hike yesterday and the woods look so great. I really enjoy living in such a beautiful setting. We saw a lot of birds, including a bright red cardinal who came right up to us asking for food. We saw some deer tracks, too. I'd love to show you my favorite bird watching lookout some day. We could take a picnic and I could show you some really pretty spots.

My latest project has gone really well, and we're almost finished. I am hoping to take a little time off when this house is done. Since becoming an architect, I don't get to ski as much as I'd like to, although Lake Placid is just about one of the best places in the world for winter sports. Skating too, as you know!

Carol says hello and really wants to meet you soon. It would be nice to see you again. Maybe you could come up on one of your vacations. You could keep up your skating here, so you wouldn't have to miss a lot of practice. I know

how important your skating is to you.
All right, champ! Until next time, and
remember you are always in our
thoughts.

                              Love,
                              Dad

Tori read the letter twice. It was the longest her father had ever sent—and the best, too. Well, actually, there hadn't been all that many letters. But how could there be? Tori thought. She and her father had only met for the first time several months earlier. Maybe her father cared more about her than she thought, especially compared to the way her mother was treating her lately. Maybe she *would* go up there and visit him soon. That would show her mother. Tori wasn't really a big nature fan, but seeing his favorite places in the woods sounded so magical. Tori wished she could be in Lake Placid right now, far away from Seneca Hills.

She started daydreaming about Lake Placid. When she'd been there for the Regionals earlier in the year, it had seemed like a really fun place. She, Jill, Dani, and Nikki had even met some cute high-school guys. True, they'd almost gotten into trouble when they'd sneaked out and met the boys at night for a snowball fight and tobogganing, but it sure had been fun. Tori thought of Tom, the guy who'd really seemed to like her. If she went to Lake Placid, she could probably see him again.

And maybe it would be a good idea to spend more time with her father. She barely knew him. Now that they had met, she thought they should have a chance to get to know each other better. After all, they had twelve years to make up for. Besides, Tori thought, it suddenly didn't seem fair that she was growing up with only one parent.

And, now that her dad had married Carol, if Tori did visit Lake Placid, she would see what it was like to have two parents. Then an idea struck her—why not *move* to Lake Placid, for good? From the sound of the letter, her father really seemed to appreciate her, and he obviously took her skating very seriously—unlike her mother. It almost seemed as if that was what he was hinting at in his letter. He'd probably be delighted to have Tori come live with him in Lake Placid. And as he'd said himself, it was one of the best places in the world for skating. They even held the Winter Olympics there once.

If Lake Placid was good enough for the Olympic Committee, she thought with a smile, then it was good enough for Tori Carsen.

9

"Tori, why don't you try some of these leg lifts," Ernie Harper said kindly during practice on Friday afternoon.

Ernie Harper was the weight trainer who worked with the Silver Blades skaters and the local hockey team, the Seneca Hills Hawks. Mr. Weiler had suggested that Tori do some extra exercise in the weight room to see if that would help her gain the height she needed for her triple toe loop. The competition was only eight days away, and Tori knew she was making no progress in improving her program. She could feel the pressure starting to mount, but she didn't seem to have any motivation. Preparing for a competition all by herself—at least without her mother's support—wasn't the same.

Tori locked her legs in place on the weight machine and began the repetitions. But her mind wandered. She released the weights with a slam and shuffled over to the water fountain.

"You're going to have to apply yourself more than that, Tori." Ernie shook his head of dark, curly hair.

Ernie was short and muscular and very dedicated to the skating club. Tori wished she could feel dedicated right now, too. But she couldn't seem to motivate herself.

"I know, Ernie," she said sadly. "It's just not my week."

"It happens to the best of us," Ernie said with a sympathetic look. "Just try your best."

Tori returned to the machines. My mom doesn't even notice that my routine is turning into a disaster, she thought as she slowly raised the weights. She's so completely into Roger Arnold that she can't even see that he's ruining our lives! Tori guessed that when her mom became Mrs. Arnold, the Carsen team would be a thing of the past. After all, then Tori would be the only Carsen left. Except for her dad.

She thought again about her plan to move to her father's in Lake Placid. She hadn't told anyone about it—not even her friends. It would be hard to leave Seneca Hills, but it had to be better than staying here.

After her weight session, Tori headed out onto the ice and tried to work on her triple toe loop again. But her leg muscles were tired after all that lifting. Finally, after she took several falls in a row, Mack drove the Zamboni onto the ice, signaling that practice was over.

Brushing the ice-shavings off her tights, Tori trudged into the locker room to change and collect her things. Then she hurried out the main door and sat with her friends on one of the benches outside the Ice Arena to wait for her mom. It would be the first time Tori's mother had picked her up from afternoon practice in days. Danielle, Nikki, and Haley's rides came, but Tori was still waiting.

She played with the zipper on her parka and scanned the road for her mother's car. Finally, ten minutes later, Mrs. Carsen pulled up and leaned over to the passenger side to open the door.

"Honey, I am so sorry," Mrs. Carsen said. "I know I'm late, but I got stuck at the store. How was practice? You look a little pale. Are you all right?"

When Tori didn't answer, Mrs. Carsen reached over to feel her forehead. "You're not too warm."

As they drove home, Tori gazed out the window and watched the houses go by. But Mrs. Carsen chattered away, not seeming to notice that Tori was not speaking. Tori closed her eyes and blocked out her mother's words. She didn't want to listen to her mom's excited gossip about the store and work. Most of all, she did not want to hear any more details about Roger "Mr. Wonderful" Arnold.

"Tori, hello!" her mother said loudly. "Are you lost in space? You haven't listened to a word I've said, have you? You know, you're really going to have to shape up if you want to come to Montreal with us."

"Montreal?" Tori repeated, confused.

"I just asked if you wanted to come to Montreal with me and Roger next weekend. Where were you?" Mrs. Carsen looked at her with concern. "Are you feeling all right? Are you coming down with something?"

"Mom," Tori said in a small voice, "the Rochester competition is next weekend. Did you forget?" Tori felt tears forming and turned her head to stare out the window so that her mother wouldn't see. Then she gazed down at her hands, twisting her gloves in her lap.

"Oh, well, I suppose I hadn't realized it was coming up so soon," her mother admitted. "Time is flying while I'm working on this project."

Tori didn't say a word. There was nothing to say. It was more obvious than ever that her mother had stopped thinking about her completely.

They pulled into the driveway, and Tori left the car without looking at her mom.

Inside the house, she dropped her schoolbooks and skate bag at the bottom of the stairs and hung up her parka in the closet. Her mother stood at the front door, watching her every move. Tori ignored her as she turned and headed up the stairs.

"Tori, where are you going?" Mrs. Carsen asked.

"Upstairs to do my homework," Tori replied in a tight voice. "Is that all right?"

"Well, I do think we should talk about this some more," Mrs. Carsen said. "But go ahead with your homework and we can talk at dinner. I'm going to have to think about this problem."

In her bedroom, Tori sat down at her white desk in front of the window. She pulled out her books, but didn't touch them. Instead she gazed out through the sheer yellow curtains. Then she removed her father's letter from its hiding place in her drawer and read it again. She hadn't told her mother about the letter, but she'd read it so many times that she practically had it memorized. Her father sounded so warm and caring, so concerned about her. Tori wished she were with him right now. She was sure he would never forget about one of her competitions—the way her mother had. This is the worst week of my life, she decided, staring out at the darkening sky.

A little while later she heard her mother calling her for dinner. The table was set for two and a steaming bowl of spaghetti sat next to a large tossed salad. Her mother brought some grated cheese to the table and set a large glass of milk at Tori's place.

Tori sat down and helped herself to some spaghetti. She couldn't quite bring herself to look at her mother's face. She thought she might cry.

"Tori, please don't feel so sad," her mother said. "I know that this has been a difficult time for you, but everything is going to be fine, I promise you."

Tori gazed up hopefully at her mom. Maybe Mrs. Carsen had changed her mind about going to Montreal, Tori thought. "You mean you won't go to Montreal?"

"Well, actually, Tori, I've been thinking about it, and I think that although the Rochester competition is important, you'll do fine without me," her mother answered. "It might even be good for you."

"Mom! How can you say that?" Tori wailed. "You always come to every competition!"

"Tori, I know. But maybe we could make an exception just this once," said her mother. "You see, Roger has already made all the arrangements. And if I am going to have the chance to get my designs into all the Arnold's Department Stores, it is going to require some sacrifices. I know it's difficult for you to understand, Tori, but this is business. It is very important to *both* of us."

"You mean both you and *Roger*," Tori said accusingly. "I don't see how you can say that a cozy weekend at a cute inn in Montreal is just business, Mom."

"Tori, I'm very sorry to hear that this is your attitude about me and Roger," Mrs. Carsen said, shaking her head. "It may be hard for you to understand at your age, but . . ." She hesitated. "But this is the first time since your father that I've felt so special about someone. You know, it's not easy being alone. And Roger and I share so many interests, and yes, business is one of them."

Tori stared at her half-eaten plate of spaghetti. She wasn't hungry anymore. In fact, she felt a little sick. Finally she looked up at her mom, tears in her eyes.

"How can you say that you've been alone?" Tori asked, her voice shaking. "What about me? Don't I count anymore?"

"Tori, of course you do. Don't you know that I love you more than anything? But it's not the same thing . . ." Mrs. Carsen's voice trailed off. "I need a little time to work things out, and I would really appreciate your understanding on this. How about it, huh, can't you help me out a bit?"

Mrs. Carsen gave Tori a little smile and reached for her hand. Tori let her mom hold her hand, but she didn't feel any better.

"Mom, how am I supposed to get to the competition without you?" she said. "And what about my dress? You're never going to have the time to make it now, and you *promised*."

"I know you're disappointed, and I'm sorry," said her mother. "But really, you have so many beautiful dresses. I should know, since I made them. I think you would look lovely in the pink chiffon. It *is* one of your favorites."

Tori thought about the dress. With its pale pink bodice and matching chiffon sleeves, it made her feel grown-up. The skirt had double layers of white and pink chiffon that moved beautifully when she skated. Of course, all her friends had seen it before, and it wouldn't be nearly as exciting as a new dress.

"And as for getting to Rochester, you can take the bus with the rest of the skaters," said Mrs. Carsen. "You said you wanted more independence, so now's your chance." She smiled. "Just think about how much fun you'll have riding up there with your friends."

Tori shrugged. "I guess," she said quietly. She felt so bad right now that she couldn't even remember what having fun felt like. The weird thing was, now it wasn't so much that she was really angry with her mother as that she felt sad and lonely. Tori felt as though she didn't have anyone to turn to. No one cared about her, she was sure of it.

But as she helped her mother tidy up the kitchen after dinner, she had a thought. There was one person who cared a lot about what happened to her— her father. And suddenly Tori wanted to talk to him right away. She had a great idea—but how to make a phone call to her dad without her mother's noticing?

A few minutes later, when Mrs. Carsen said she was going upstairs to take a long bath, Tori grabbed the opportunity. When Tori heard the bathwater stop running, and she was sure her mom was in the tub, she picked up the phone and dialed the operator. She got her father's number from Lake Placid information and dialed it quickly.

"Hello, Dad?" Tori said when she heard her father answer the phone. "It's me, Tori," she said a little awkwardly.

"Tori! What a surprise! How are you?" Her father sounded happy to hear from her.

"I'm okay," Tori lied. She tried to sound cheerful

as she shared her plan. "Listen, um, I was wondering if you thought Rochester was too far away from where you are in Lake Placid, or if maybe you wanted to come and see my competition next weekend?"

"That's a great idea," said her father. "I'm so touched that you thought of me. Carol and I don't have any plans, so sure, we'd love to see you compete."

"Really?" said Tori excitedly.

"Of course," said her father enthusiastically. He paused. "But what about your mother? You don't think she'll mind if I come?"

"Mom can't make it," Tori explained.

"Well then, Carol and I will be happy to step in for her and be your cheering section," he said. "I'll make a reservation at a hotel, and we'll see you up there."

When Tori hung up, she felt much better. Calling her father had definitely been the right thing to do. It was clear that her mother felt Tori was just in the way. But her father obviously couldn't wait to see her again, and when she did see him, Tori would give him the good news. She was coming home with him to Lake Placid! She would move in with her father for good, right after the Rochester competition. Nothing was going to stop her!

10

Saturday afternoon at the end of the freestyle practice session, Tori brushed the ice off her tights after
falling for what felt like the millionth time while trying to perfect her triple toe loop. She was beginning
to get more consistent, but she was still unsure about
nailing it in time for the competition. And Blake had
been too busy working with Haley and Patrick to
squeeze in any extra time with her. If only she had
started working seriously on the jump a little earlier.

She headed for the boards and felt a tug on the red
skirt of her skating dress. She whirled around and
saw Haley, Danielle, and Nikki.

"You're it!" Haley screamed, laughing as she
zoomed away.

Before she even realized what she was doing, Tori
took off after her. The girls sped around the ice for

a few minutes, laughing and yelling while they played a quick game of freeze tag. Only after Mack fired up the Zamboni to clean the rink for the public session did they charge off the ice.

"Tori," Danielle said as they clunked into the locker room on their skate guards, "we think you need to come to the mall with us today."

"What?" said Tori. "You mean now?"

"Yep," agreed Haley. "Right now. This very minute."

"It's all set," said Danielle. "My grandmother is going to drop us off, and Haley's mom is going to take us home later. You were going to drive with us anyway, so it's perfect."

"Come on," said Nikki. "It'll be fun."

"Yeah, and you look like you could use a little fun," added Haley. "What's up? You seem kind of down lately."

"Oh, well, I guess I'm just worried about my routine for Rochester," Tori said evasively.

"What you need is a break, then," said Danielle. "A few hours where you don't even have to *think* about skating."

Right now, with everything that's going on, skating is the *last* thing on my mind, thought Tori. But she said only, "Okay, guys, that sounds great. Thanks. I'll leave a message for my mom and meet you outside in a minute."

After calling home and talking to the answering machine, Tori pulled on her blue parka and pushed through the doors of the Ice Arena to join her friends. I'm really going to miss this place when I'm in Lake Placid, she thought to herself.

A little while later, Grandma Panati left them outside the mall and reminded them not to make Mrs. Arthur wait when she came to pick them up. The girls all hopped out of the car and headed inside.

Tori scanned the rows and rows of stores, realizing that this might be one of the last times she would see one of her favorite places in the whole world.

"Let's go to Super Sundaes," suggested Nikki. "I'm dying for a scoop of double-dark-chocolate frozen yogurt."

"Not for me," sighed Danielle.

"You can have a fruit sorbet," Haley said firmly. "Come on, let's go."

After the girls got their cones, they wandered around looking in the store windows. Tori saw a pair of shoes she liked in Canady's, one of the most popular clothing stores in Seneca Hills, and at the News Hut Nikki picked up a skating magazine that Jill had asked her to get. Poor Jill was still on crutches, but she was supposed to get her cast removed pretty soon.

Then they passed the site of the new Arnold's Department Store. The large plate glass windows were papered over, and a sign read COMING SOON— ARNOLD'S, FOR ALL YOUR SHOPPING NEEDS.

"Hey, Tori, do you think your mom is in there?" asked Haley, licking her strawberry swirl yogurt.

"Maybe." Tori shrugged.

"Should we go in and ask?" suggested Nikki.

"No. If she is, she's way too busy to be bothered," Tori said, not wanting to see her mom with Mr. Arnold again.

"Yeah, I guess she must be busy," Danielle agreed. "I haven't seen your mom at practice for almost the entire week."

"That's because the only thing she does anymore is work on Arnold's Department Stores," Tori blurted.

"Wow, Tori, you definitely seem like you're not into your mom doing this Arnold's thing at all," said Nikki.

"Yeah," said Haley. "What's going on?"

Looking at her three best friends' worried faces, Tori couldn't keep it in any longer.

"Everything! And it's all because of that awful Roger Arnold," she burst out. "You won't believe what's happening. He's taking up *all* of my mom's time!" She paused. "And he's just *using* her, and she doesn't even see it!"

"What do you mean?" asked Haley with concern.

"Using her how, Tori?" asked Nikki.

"Are you sure?" asked Danielle.

"Positive," Tori declared, starting to warm up to the subject. She'd kept everything in for so long that the words tumbled out. "*Roger* is making my mom spend all her time working on clothes for his stupid store. Not only for this store, but for *all* the Arnold's Department Stores, and now he's taking her to Montreal next weekend to do more work up there! I know all he really cares about is using Corinne Carsen designs to bring more people into his stupid stores, but *she* thinks he wants to marry her. And you should see the way they act together! It's unbelievable. They're together all the time, talking about business and teamwork."

Tori paused, out of breath. Now she had tears in her eyes, and the other girls were staring at her, obviously shocked. She took a deep breath and went on.

"And he's purposely trying to get between us, because he knows I can see what's going on," she said. Then she thought of something. "He left his last wife and I know he'll leave my mom once she does all this work to make his business better." Tori knew she was stretching the truth, but she had to get her point across. "Anyway," she finished, wiping a tear, "I can't watch him do this to her, so . . . I'm going to go live with my dad."

The other girls were stunned. They looked at one other for a moment before they started firing questions at Tori.

"Wait a minute," said Haley. "Your mom is going to *marry* Mr. Arnold? And you didn't tell us?"

"He left his last wife, and he's going to marry your mom and then leave her, too?" added Nikki.

"What makes you so sure about this, Tori?" asked Danielle. "And when did your dad say you should move to Lake Placid?"

"And what about us? Are you really going to leave Silver Blades and everything?" asked Haley sadly.

Tori nodded and hung her head, unable to look at her friends. "I know," she said. "I'm going to hate leaving you guys, but the way things are with my mom and Mr. Arnold, I *can't* stay. As soon as I see my dad in Rochester, we'll work out the details and that'll be that."

"You're going too fast Tori," Haley objected. "You mean you haven't even spoken with your dad yet?"

"Oh, I spoke with him," Tori said truthfully. "But not about when, exactly, I would move to Lake Placid. Actually, he just thinks I'm coming up for a vacation sometime soon."

"Tori, I don't know," said Danielle cautiously. "It sounds like you might be going a little overboard here. Don't you think you should clear things with your dad before you go making plans to move in?"

"Yeah," said Nikki. "How do you know he's ready to have you come live with him?"

"Believe me," Tori said confidently, "he is. You should read the letter he wrote me. You see, he's so happy to have finally met me this year that he wants to make up for lost time. Besides, when he hears what's happening, he'll have no choice. He couldn't possibly leave me stranded here in Seneca Hills when my mom is running around the country with Mr. Arnold."

"Tori," Haley said doubtfully, "the whole thing sounds kind of strange. I mean, I can't imagine that your mom would change that much, just from one day to the next. And what about your skating career? She's totally involved with that."

"Oh, really," said Tori bitterly. "You mean because of the way she's been at practice watching my every move recently? Or the way she's been working on my new dress? Forget it. My mom doesn't care anymore."

"Well, when is your mom getting married to Mr. Arnold, Tori?" Nikki asked, glancing at Haley. "Are you going to be in the wedding?"

"I don't know," Tori lied. "He's going to settle down here in Seneca Hills, and I guess they'll make plans after the store opens."

"Wow. This sure is some news," commented Danielle.

"Yeah, but keep it to yourselves, okay?" Tori said worriedly. "I haven't told my mom yet about moving to Lake Placid with my dad, and I don't want her to hear about it the wrong way. This is just between us, promise?"

"We promise," Haley swore.

Nikki and Danielle nodded their agreement.

"But I still think you better talk to your dad some more about this," said Danielle. "He might not be as ready as you think to have a daughter move in with him."

"Really, Tori, you and your dad barely know each other," Haley said, her green eyes very serious.

"And he has a new wife, too, right?" Nikki pointed out. "If you went to live with them you'd have a stepmother, you know."

Tori was starting to get really upset with her friends. They didn't understand how bad things were. She felt more alone than ever.

"You guys can say what you like," she retorted, "but I'm definitely moving to Lake Placid to live with my dad. And with all the bad things going on with my mom and that awful Roger Arnold, I would think that my best friends could try to understand."

"Tori! We do understand!" Haley protested.

"Yeah," said Danielle. "We're your best friends, and we care about you."

"We're just sad that you're going to be leaving Seneca Hills," said Nikki. "But of course you can count on us."

"Right," Haley added quietly. "We'll always be here for you. Even if you do move to Lake Placid."

"Thanks, guys," Tori said. "I'm sorry if I snapped at you. I'm just having a hard time right now." She brightened. "Hey, what do you think, maybe I can see that cute guy Tom once I live in Lake Placid. Won't that be great?"

"We're ready to visit, that's for sure!" Danielle said excitedly.

"I'd love to skate there again. It was so much fun at the North Atlantic Regionals!" exclaimed Nikki.

As the girls studied the windows of their favorite shops, Tori thought about how much she would miss times like this with her friends from Silver Blades. But they would come visit her in Lake Placid—a lot. And her father would be so happy to have her home with him at last. For the first time in weeks, Tori was looking forward to the Rochester competition.

11

Tori stood on the ice, listening to Mr. Weiler talk to her about her program. She couldn't believe how fast the week had passed. She was so busy thinking about her plans to move to Lake Placid that hardly anything else seemed to matter. And now here it was, the day before the Silver Blades skaters were to leave for Rochester. She couldn't help wishing that she had spent more time working on her program.

Mr. Weiler seemed to be thinking the same thing. "Tori, I just don't know what to say," he continued. "It's obvious that your heart is not in your skating. We leave for the competition tomorrow, and you are clearly not ready."

Tori fidgeted with the hem of her lavender skating skirt and looked up into the bleachers out of habit.

Then she remembered that her mother wasn't there, that she had left that morning for Montreal. Tori would spend the night at the Panatis', and Mrs. Panati would chaperon both her and Danielle at the competition. At least I don't have to listen to my mom criticize me, *too*, Tori thought. She tried to look apologetic as Mr. Weiler went on.

"Your triple toe loop has gotten worse, not better," he said, "so I guess we are just going to have to cross our fingers you'll land it in competition. You may have to change it to a double toe loop. Let's work on the double Lutz–double toe loop combination."

Tori stared down at the ice. She hated to disappoint Mr. Weiler.

"Okay," he said, "Let me see you do the double Lutz and then go into the double toe loop. Let's see what we can save from this program Blake worked on for you."

"All right, Mr. Weiler," Tori said, giving him a little smile.

But Mr. Weiler was definitely not in a good mood. Boy, he's really mad, Tori thought as she looked at his frowning face. Okay, concentrate, I have to concentrate, she told herself.

She tried to keep her focus, but as soon as she imagined performing her routine, a picture of her dad, sitting in the bleachers at the competition watching her, popped into her mind. She shivered a little with excitement. She couldn't wait to surprise him with the good news.

Tori powered up for the combination, first taking off for the double Lutz from her left back outside edge. She planted her right toe pick and sprang into the air, rotating counterclockwise into the double loop. Landing smoothly, she immediately bent her right knee and lifted, but she landed after only one and a half revolutions. Her recovery was poor, and she circled back to start over.

"Tori, what is it?" said Mr. Weiler. "I thought you were going to really work on this last week, but I see I was wrong. I'm not even sure if you can pull off this double, let alone the triple we've been working on."

Tori hung her head and took a deep breath. Mr. Weiler is right, she thought. I'm not ready for this, and I begged Blake to choreograph this routine for me.

Tori tried again, this time keeping everything out of her mind but the image of gliding to a triumphant finish. And it worked. She completed the entire program with no mistakes and skated over to Mr. Weiler with a smile on her face.

"I don't know why you're stopping now, Tori," Mr. Weiler warned her. "Just because you can do this routine once doesn't mean you've got it down. I want to see you do the same thing three more times, and I want to see a little style out there."

Tori knew Mr. Weiler was only trying to help her, but she couldn't help feeling frustrated. This is going to be tough, she thought. She skated through her routine three more times as Mr. Weiler directed.

While she did not make any more mistakes, she knew her work was still sloppy. Mr. Weiler called her over.

"Well, Tori," he said, "technically, you did it. But I can see Blake was wrong to push you with such an advanced program. Perhaps you can concentrate on the finishing touches—placing your hands and extending your fingertips on the landings. At the very least we can manage to look more graceful up at Rochester." He sighed. "Okay, enough for now. I hope we can polish this some more when we get to the competition, but I'm afraid it's going to be too little, too late."

He left her standing at the boards feeling miserable. She knew she deserved everything he had said, but she still hated to be criticized like that. She told herself that things would get back to normal when she was in Lake Placid with her dad. She wouldn't be working with Mr. Weiler after this anyway.

As she slipped on her guards and Silver Blades warm-up jacket, Nikki and Danielle came up to her.

"Wow, Mr. Weiler sure gave you a hard time, huh?" said Danielle gently. "He's not usually like that."

"I know," Tori agreed. "But it's my own fault. I keep thinking about moving in with my dad, and I just can't seem to concentrate."

"I know what you mean," said Nikki. "My mom is going to have the baby any day now, maybe any *minute*! It's so hard for me to think about skating. I'm so nervous! But my dad promised to call me in Rochester as soon as there's any news."

"Well, you two sure have exciting lives," Danielle teased. "I'm sure glad Haley is around. She and I can just keep on with our boring skating lives, trying to get into the Olympics and worrying about being champions."

Nikki and Tori laughed as they put their arms around Danielle, and the three girls headed for the locker room.

"Hey, champ," Tori teased Danielle, "what do you think your grandmother's making us for dinner before the big competition?"

"Beats me." Danielle grinned. "But whatever it is, I'm sure I'll want seconds."

Inside the locker room, the girls changed out of their skating clothes. Tori packed her lavender practice dress into the suitcase she had with her for the trip to Rochester. When she had packed, she had managed to slip in a few extra outfits, but not enough to arouse her mother's suspicions. She planned to send for the rest of her things once she got settled in with her dad in Lake Placid.

After dinner at the Panatis', the girls and Nicholas helped clear the table and clean the kitchen. Tori washed the plates, Danielle dried, and Nicholas put them away in the cabinet.

"Hey, squirt," Nicholas teased Danielle, "when are you going to be tall enough to do this instead of me?"

"Nicholas, you'll do anything to get out of chores, won't you?" Danielle shot back, then whispered to Tori, "I wish I were taller."

"I like being petite," said Tori. "But my dad is pretty tall. I'll grow more for sure."

"I think it's time for these growing girls to get into bed." Mrs. Panati poked her head through the kitchen door. "I really appreciate you and Tori helping out, but Nicholas and I can finish. You two are going to have a long day."

Nicholas groaned. "Maybe I should take up figure skating." He wrapped a dishtowel around his waist. "What do you think of my tutu?"

"Skating skirt," Danielle corrected. "Tutus are for ballerinas."

Nicholas shrugged. "What's the difference?"

Danielle rolled her eyes. "Come on, Tori, let's go."

The two girls headed into Danielle's cozy room, with its twin beds covered in matching rainbow-colored afghans. They changed into their pajamas and slipped under the covers. Danielle reached for the light, then stopped and turned to Tori.

"Tori," Danielle said.

"Yes, Dani," Tori answered, rolling over to look at her friend.

"Are you nervous about the competition?"

"Yeah," Tori admitted, "I am. But I'm much more nervous about seeing my dad," she added quietly.

"You know," said Danielle softly, "you can always change your mind."

"What?" Tori said.

"About moving to Lake Placid," said Danielle. "I mean, you haven't even really told your dad about it yet. Or your mom."

Tori thought a moment. It would be hard to leave Seneca Hills and her friends at Silver Blades behind. Maybe moving to Lake Placid wasn't such a great idea, considering.

"No, Dani," she said firmly. "I know it's the right thing." She rolled over. "Now, let's get some rest, okay?"

"Okay," said Danielle, turning out the light.

There was silence for a moment.

"Oh," said Danielle, "one more thing."

"What?" said Tori.

"What should we do about the baby present for Nikki's mom?" Danielle asked. "I mean, she's going to have the baby really soon, and we still haven't thought of anything."

"I don't know," said Tori. "Maybe we should wait to see if it's a girl or a boy. Then we can get the right sort of gift."

Then she realized something. "Anyway, you should probably count me out," she said quietly. "After all, I won't be around to pick out anything with you guys."

"Yeah," said Danielle softly. "I guess you won't. Good night, Tori."

" 'Night, Dani," said Tori.

In what seemed like no time at all, the alarm was ringing for them to wake up and catch the bus for Rochester. It was only six o'clock in the morning, so Nicholas and Mr. Panati were still asleep. Grandma Panati whipped up a quick breakfast for the girls and Mrs. Panati, then wished them luck as she waved good-bye. Soon Mrs. Panati, Danielle, and Tori were waiting outside the Seneca Hills Ice Arena with the rest of the Silver Blades skaters.

After the bus was loaded up and the skaters were on their way, Tori found herself staring out the window, thinking about her father and her plans to talk to him at the competition. A nudge from Nikki, who was sitting next to her, interrupted her thoughts.

"Thinking about your father again?" Nikki guessed.

"Yes," Tori admitted. "It's funny but I've really only seen him that once, and I'm wondering if I'll even be able to recognize him."

"Don't worry," said Nikki. "I'm sure he'll recognize you."

"Yeah, I guess I'm a little nervous," said Tori, gazing out the window again.

"It's not too late to change your mind, Tori," Nikki said quietly. "You could think about it awhile longer. There's really no rush."

Tori sighed, exasperated. Why was everyone acting as if she were making the wrong decision? She was moving in with her father and that was that. Couldn't her friends see that she had no choice?

"Look," she said, "I've made up my mind. I know you guys are trying to help, but this is the right thing for me to do. Everyone is going to be much happier this way, I'm sure."

Nikki didn't look very convinced, but she put her arm around Tori.

"Okay, I guess you know best, Tori," Nikki said. "I hope you'll be as happy with your new family as I know I'll be with mine."

Tori smiled at her friend, but she couldn't help feeling a little funny. The idea of a new family was so strange. But she'd adjust. Life with her dad would be great, she reassured herself. The longer she thought about it, the more sense it made. But what was that nagging feeling in the pit of her stomach every time she thought about telling her mom? She pushed that thought aside. Her dad would help her to explain everything—she was sure of it.

12

As the Silver Blades bus approached Rochester, a ripple of energy ran through the group. Tori was excited but nervous. Normally she would be thinking ahead to the competition later that afternoon, wondering how she and the other members of Silver Blades would do. But now she had too many things on her mind.

Then, in the lobby of the large Rochester sports complex, while Mr. Weiler and Kathy Bart checked in the team, Tori caught sight of a bunch of red-and-black warm-up jackets. The Blade Runners! Of course their rival skating club would be here! Tori had forgotten all about them. And about Carla Benson, who would be here, too. Tori had a big rivalry going with Carla. Tori looked around but didn't see her. But Carla's here somewhere, Tori thought grimly. Suddenly she began to wish that she had worked harder on her routine—a lot harder.

The skaters settled into their rooms at the hotel next to the ice arena before their practice sessions started. Tori and Danielle shared a room, with Nikki and Haley in a room next door and Danielle's and Haley's moms in another room on the other side.

As Tori and Danielle finished unpacking, there was a knock at their door. It was Haley and Nikki.

"You guys," said Nikki, "I am so completely nervous about waiting to hear from Dad about the baby that I've got to *do* something or I'll go crazy! Let's check out the rink and the locker rooms."

Poor Nikki, thought Tori as the girls left the hotel, I know how hard it is to be nervous about your family.

But once they pushed through the arena's doors and Tori felt the blast of cold air from the ice on her face, she relaxed. That cold, crisp feeling always made her feel strong.

The girls took a quick tour of the place and were approaching the locker room when they ran into Sarge.

"Hope you girls are feeling up to form," Kathy said. "You could cut the tension in this rink with a knife."

Tori glanced past Kathy where she stood near the doorway of the locker room. She saw someone leaning into the room, her back to them. The girl wore a Blade Runners jacket. There was only one skater who would be checking things out so early, Tori thought, starting to feel anxious all over again.

Kathy followed Tori's eyes. With a smile, the coach turned back to Tori. "Looks like Carla Benson is here," she said pointedly. "Well, see you for practice in two hours, ladies."

Tori gritted her teeth and turned to her friends. "Come on," she said loudly. "We have a right to check out the locker room, no matter who is blocking the door."

Her chin in the air, Tori sailed ahead, and Danielle, Haley, and Nikki fell in right behind her. They stepped over Carla's bag and into the room.

Tori pointedly stopped in front of the big mirror by the door to adjust her warm-up jacket and leggings. Pushing a stray blond curl out of her eyes, she looked up to see Carla staring at her in the mirror. The two girls' steely faces did not change, but each knew the other was there and ready to skate.

Outside with Nikki and Danielle, Tori felt less confident, wishing for the tenth time that she had practiced more. This is going to be so tough, and it's all going to be happening in front of my dad, too, she thought. What a mess! What would Mom say if she were here? *Think like a champ and you'll skate like a champ*. And that's exactly what I will do.

An hour and a half later, after lunch at the cafe in the sports complex, Tori reported to the rink for her thirty minutes of practice time and found herself skating under Blake's watchful eye. Careful to avoid the other skaters, Tori made a small circle of backward crossovers and then stepped with her left foot into a camel spin. As she gained speed in her spin, she lifted her right leg into an arabesque and pulled both her arms back along her body. She did her spin perfectly and then began skating backward again, looking over her shoulder for the spot where she would plant her toe pick to leap into the air for her double Lutz. She spun two full rotations and landed gracefully, remembering to smile and extend her fingertips. She was completely absorbed in her skating for the first time in weeks and continued to the end of the practice session with grace and style.

She wished she could perform her long program right now. But today the skaters were only competing in the short program, which was a basic routine Tori had skated dozens of times before. She would perform her new routine tomorrow.

She could tell from Blake's smile that he thought she had done well, too. "Now *that's* the skater I created this choreography for," he complimented her. "Tori, if you can perform as well for the judges as you did just now, we'll be okay. Of course, I would have been happier with the triple, but you and Mr. Weiler can work on that for the next time."

For the first time in days, Tori felt happy. It seemed like so long since she'd heard a good word about her skating from anybody. Then she spotted Carla Benson executing a flawless triple toe loop on the other side of the rink. Tori flushed. That was supposed to be *her* move to show off at Rochester.

Tori needed to concentrate on her skating. As her mother always said, there were plenty of other skaters who would be happy to count her out of the competition as they moved onward and upward—skaters like Carla Benson.

As Tori put on her skate guards, she spotted her father waving to her from behind the barriers. Beside him was a black-haired woman dressed in a hot pink parka trimmed with silver fake fur that streamed out all around her face. Yuck! thought Tori, I wouldn't be caught dead in that ugly jacket. And then she realized—that must be Carol, his wife!

Oh no, thought Tori, as Carol jumped up and down and waved. Everybody in the rink must be staring at her. But then she reminded herself that Carol was her stepmother. That meant they had to get along. Well, Tori said to herself, trying to make the best of the situation, at least she's enthusiastic.

Tori stepped off the ice and walked over to them. "Hi!" she exclaimed. "How long have you been here?"

"Long enough to see that impressive practice session," her father answered, managing an awkward hug. There was a pause, and then he pushed Carol forward. "Tori, this is Carol, my wife. And your stepmother, I guess. Carol, meet Tori."

Carol stretched out her hand with a smile.

"Hi," Tori said shyly, taking Carol's hand.

"Hi there, Tori," Carol squeaked. She had a funny

voice, sort of high and as if she was out of breath. "I'm *so* happy to meet you. Your daddy has told me *so* much about you."

"Oh, uh, thanks," Tori answered, not sure what she should say.

"Well, we don't want to interrupt your practice," said Tori's father. "We just wanted to let you know that we're here."

"Oh, you're not interrupting," said Tori. "I mean, I'm finished. You know, for now. And the competition doesn't start for about two more hours."

"Well, then, do you have time to go for a bite or something?" asked her father.

"I already ate lunch," Tori said. "But we could go to the coffee shop for something to drink. I have almost an hour before I have to get ready."

"Super!" Carol exclaimed in her high voice. "How about a hot chocolate? How does that sound, Tori? Yummy?"

Yummy? Tori thought. How old does Carol think I am, five? Be nice, she reminded herself. After all, Carol *is* your stepmother. It's important to get along.

"Sure, that would be great," said Tori. "Just let me tell Mrs. Panati where I'm going."

Tori found Danielle's mom waiting near the locker room and told her that she would be with her dad in the coffee shop. As Tori pointed him out to Mrs. Panati, she felt proud of how tall and handsome he looked in his dark blue parka.

Joining her father and Carol at the table, Tori felt better than she had in two weeks. Her practice session had gone much more smoothly than she expected, and now here she was with her new family. Tori wondered when to tell her dad the great news. Maybe it would be better to wait until they were alone. She wasn't sure what to think about Carol yet.

The waiter brought over their hot chocolates. Tori took a sip, but no one spoke. Then suddenly they all began talking at the same time. The three of them laughed nervously. Tori waited and Carol began, "So, Tori, tell us, what other winter sports do you like?"

"I pretty much only have time for skating," Tori explained. "But I love tobogganing and anything having to do with the snow."

"That's good," said her father. "Carol and I are major ski buffs. That's how we met, actually. I gave Carol her first skiing lessons."

"Oh, you should have seen how bad I was." Carol giggled. She stirred her hot chocolate, still smiling. With her long, black hair and green eyes, she was very pretty, Tori observed. If only she were a better dresser.

"Carol has really improved," Mr. Carsen said. "In fact, we like to travel to different ski spots around the world for our vacations. Last year we went to Chile. It's winter there when it's summer here, so we had the best of both worlds."

"The mountains there are *very* tall," Carol said excitedly. "This year we plan to go to the Alps. We haven't been there for a while."

"It sounds pretty exciting," Tori said. "It must be great to travel around the world all the time." But she wondered if they'd let her stay all by herself while they were gone.

"Oh, don't get us wrong, Tori," said her father. "It's expensive to do all that traveling, so when we're home in Lake Placid, we work plenty hard, believe me."

"I'm a dance instructor," Carol explained brightly. "I especially enjoyed watching you practice your little moves out there, Tori. I noticed that you used your hands very gracefully. It must be a lot like dancing."

Tori bristled at the words "little moves," but managed to smile at the compliment. "Yes," she said. "There is a lot of dance in skating. I have friends who take ballet to improve their skating."

They talked a few minutes more, and then Tori noticed it was time for her to return to the rink. She had to change into her competition dress. She was in the first group of skaters to compete, and the competition would be starting soon.

When Tori's dad stood up to pay the check, Carol turned to her. "Your daddy is *very* proud of you, Tori," she said. "Your mommy must have done a *super* job raising you. And I'm very happy we got this chance to meet. I hope we can become better friends someday." She smiled. "Maybe you can even come up for a little visit."

Tori smiled back, but she felt slightly uncomfortable being alone with Carol. And what did Carol mean by "someday" and "little visit"? How would Carol feel when she found out that Tori planned to move to Lake Placid permanently? Before Tori had to say anything else, Mr. Carsen was back and they left for the rink together.

Fifteen minutes later, Tori glided onto the ice with her group for her warm-up before the short mandatory programs. She felt relieved to get back on familiar ground, just her and the other skaters. She glanced over at Danielle to see how she was doing, but her friend seemed totally relaxed and focused. The five-minute warm-up ended too quickly.

Now Tori and the others waited for their turn to compete in the hallway leading to the rink. When your turn comes, just focus, Tori reminded herself. Try to give in to the music and don't think about anything else. But as she tried to clear her mind, she spotted Carla Benson standing to her left with the rest of the Blade Runners. Rather than look at Carla, Tori gazed down and smoothed her skating skirt.

A second later, she heard her name announced on the PA system.

Tori skated to the center and took up her position. The music, a medley from *The Sound of Music*, started slowly, and Tori glided down the center of the ice in a dramatic spiral. She raised her right leg high over her head. As the tempo increased, she whirled into a series of jumps. Her short program wasn't too much of a challenge, since she'd done it many times before. The tough part of the competition would be tomorrow, when she performed Blake's new routine.

Still, when she ended with a graceful layback spin, Tori knew she had not skated her best. While she had made no big mistakes, her performance had been wooden and automatic, with none of the charm and grace she usually tried to bring to her skating. She supposed she must have been thinking about meeting with her father and Carol.

But did it really affect me so badly? she wondered, feeling panicky.

How would she feel tomorrow, when she had much tougher things to face—a more difficult routine, telling her father the news, and saying good-bye to her friends from Silver Blades forever.

Tori slept badly that night, tossing and turning. It didn't help that she had to listen to Danielle's smooth, even, heavy breathing from the next bed. *How can she sleep so soundly?* Tori wondered. *But then again,* she reminded herself, *Danielle performed an excellent short program and doesn't have nearly as much on her mind as I do.*

Everything's happening all at once, Tori thought. *Between thinking about my routine and thinking about my dad, I feel like I'm going to explode. Maybe if I can wait until* after *I finish competing to talk to him, I'll be able to handle everything better.*

Finally, it was morning, and Tori, Nikki, Haley, Alex, Patrick, and Danielle sat in the sports complex's café eating breakfast.

"So, Tori, aren't you proud of Dani?" Nikki asked.

"She did really well yesterday. Maybe Silver Blades will bring home a lot of medals from Rochester this year."

"Yeah, Dani." Tori sighed. "You were great. I wish I could say the same."

Nikki and Danielle exchanged glances.

"Wasn't that your dad you were talking to right before the short program?" asked Nikki.

Tori nodded. "He came with his wife, Carol."

"Did you talk to him about moving in with him?" asked Danielle.

"No," Tori admitted. "It just didn't seem like the right time."

"I understand why you wouldn't want to bring it up then, right before you had to skate," said Nikki. "In fact, maybe talking to them threw off your skating."

"I was thinking the same thing yesterday," Tori sighed. "It was really hard meeting Carol for the first time while I was supposed to be focusing on my program."

"So how was she? Do you like her?" asked Danielle.

"She's okay," Tori said without much enthusiasm. "She's a dance instructor, and she was interested in my skating."

Haley leaned forward. "Is that all?"

"I don't know if I really want to talk about this right now, guys," Tori said, picking up her tray, her bagel only half eaten and her oatmeal hardly touched. The truth was, the meeting with her father wasn't as warm and easy as she expected. And she was embarrassed by Carol. Her father's wife seemed like such an airhead. Tori certainly didn't want her friends to meet her. "I really need to stretch out and get my mind focused," she said. "So maybe I should take your advice and talk about this later, after skating, okay?" Tori smiled, but she felt very tense already.

"Sure, Tori," Nikki said, glacing at Haley.

"Fine with me," Haley agreed. "We'll see you in an hour or so."

Tori waved to her friends and headed up to her hotel room to relax before the big competition later that morning.

As she laced up her skates in the locker room an hour and a half later, Tori wondered if her father and Carol would be waiting for her before she had to perform her long program. There was no way she'd be able to concentrate on her skating if she stopped to talk to them. Just the sight of them would remind her of everything that was going on.

Tori made a decision. If her father and Carol were there, she would tell them nicely, but firmly, that skating had to be her first priority today. After all, if she was going to live with them, they would have to understand that for her, skating came first. Then she had a thought. What if her skating schedule was a problem for her father and Carol? With their busy work schedules and traveling around the world for the best skiing, it didn't sound as though there would be much time for taking Tori to and from the rink and competitions.

Tori put on her skate guards and checked her outfit in the mirror. She smoothed her hair and fingered the hem of her pale pink chiffon dress. The pretty outfit her mother had made last year for the long program had brought her luck then. Maybe it would bring her luck now.

Tori thought about how awful Carol's hot pink parka had looked yesterday. Her own mother would have never worn something so bright. Carol had no fashion sense at all. Well, maybe we can work on that, Tori thought, but somehow she doubted Carol would take the advice of a thirteen-year-old.

Sure enough, as Tori waited by the side of the rink a little while later for her group to be called for the five-minute practice session before the long program portion of the competition, she heard someone shouting her name. She glanced up to see Carol waving and jumping up and down in the bleachers to get her attention. Her father was closer, by the barriers. "Hi, Tori!" he called out.

Tori blushed as the skaters around her turned their heads. "Hi, dad," she began, walking quickly toward him.

"Carol and I are so looking forward to your long program today," he said.

"I can see that," Tori said a bit sharply as Carol hurried up to them.

"Hi, Tori," Carol exclaimed as she gave Tori a big pink hug.

Tori blew some of the strands of fake fur out of her mouth before moving away from Carol and her hot pink parka.

"Listen, you guys," Tori began. "I have only five minutes to warm up, and then I have to concentrate on competing. I can't talk now. I'll see you afterwards, okay?"

Without waiting for an answer, she hurried away. Her warm-up group was beginning to file onto the ice. Tori pulled off her skate guards. When she got to her space on the rink with Mr. Weiler, she was fidgety. Mr. Weiler looked at her with concern.

"What's going on, Tori? Who are those people?" he asked.

"That's my father and stepmother," Tori answered.

"Oh, I see," said Mr. Weiler. "Where's your mother?"

"She couldn't make it to this one," Tori answered. "She had to go to Montreal. That's why I took the bus." But if she *were* here, Tori added to herself, she'd know how to act at a competition—unlike her father and Carol.

"Uh, okay," Mr. Weiler said. "Let's get started."

Tori did her practice warm-up with ease, but when she got to her double Lutz–double toe loop combination, she faltered and made only one and a half revolutions on the final jump. She and Mr. Weiler exchanged worried glances, but the warm-up time was over, and Tori's group had to leave the ice.

"Let me give you some advice," said Mr. Weiler. "Just think about skating. Don't get involved in anything else. I have a lot of faith in you. If you go out there and have a good time, you *will* skate well, I promise you."

Tori was grateful that Mr. Weiler believed in her, even though she hadn't landed the combination. Maybe if she could just let everything else go, she would have a chance to do well after all. She had to focus on the ice and the music.

A few minutes later Tori stood in the hall leading to the ice, waiting for her turn and nervously smoothing the skirt of her pink chiffon outfit. It was a beautiful dress, she knew. The fitted bodice brought out the elegant lines of her movements, especially in the spins. But she was very tense, much more so than usual. She tried to calm herself down, but it was no use.

Tori glanced around at the other competitors. Everyone was thinking about the competition. The tension was electrifying.

Tori wished more than ever that she had put in the time to perfect her routine back in Seneca Hills. She would feel so much better now if she could skate out there with confidence. But she wasn't used to working on her skating all alone. I guess this is how it's going to be from now on, though, she reminded herself. After all, my dad doesn't exactly know enough about skating to help me practice, and I certainly don't want Carol involved in my skating.

As Tori watched her rival Carla Benson perform a beautiful routine on the ice, she felt even worse.

A hand on her shoulder made Tori jump. She turned to see—her mother! Mrs. Carsen stood with a small smile on her face. Roger Arnold was behind her. Tori couldn't believe it. For once, she was speechless.

"Hi, honey," Mrs. Carsen said in her raspy voice. "Surprised?"

"M-Mom," Tori sputtered. "What are you doing here?"

"We cut our trip short," her mother answered.

Roger Arnold smiled and gave a little wave.

"You did?" asked Tori, amazed. "Why?"

"Why do you think, silly?" said her mother. "So we could be here for you. Listen, I know you're about to go on, so I'll talk to you later, but I wanted to wish you luck."

Tori couldn't believe her ears. She knew the trip to Montreal was really important to her mom.

Mrs. Carsen leaned over to give her a quick kiss and turned to go. But as she and Roger walked back to the bleachers, Tori's dad and Carol burst into the hallway. Tori's mom and dad bumped right into each other at the door.

Oh boy, thought Tori. Here we go. She hurried to where her mother, father, Roger, and Carol stood awkwardly at the door, all looking at each other.

"James!" Mrs. Carsen said in a shocked voice. "What are *you* doing here?"

"Watching my daughter compete," Mr. Carsen replied. "Tori invited me and Carol to come see her."

"She did?" Mrs. Carsen asked, astonished.

"She certainly did," Tori's father replied. "In fact, Corinne, I must say I'm a little surprised to see *you* here."

"What do you mean?" her mother said defensively. "Of course I'm here. I'm her *mother*."

"Oh, hello there!" said Carol in her high voice. She put out her hand. "I'm Carol. I've so enjoyed meeting Tori."

Mrs. Carsen ignored her and turned to Tori. "Why didn't you say anything to me about this?" she demanded.

Tori opened her mouth, but nothing came out. She gaped at her parents. This wasn't the way it was supposed to turn out at all. She had wanted to wait until she had finished skating.

"Tori?" said her mother again. "What's going on?"

Finally Tori couldn't keep it in any longer. She looked from her mother to Roger to her father to Carol. "I'm going to move in with Dad!" she blurted out.

She felt tears start as she watched the expressions on her parents' faces change from disbelief to shock. Both her mother and father looked confused and upset.

"James!" Tori's mother exploded. "Was this your

idea? Because if so, I hardly think this is an appropriate—"

"Hold on, Corinne," her father said sharply. "Stop jumping to conclusions. I'm as surprised about this as you are, believe me."

"Okay now, everyone," Carol squeaked. "Let's all just calm down and see if we can work this out."

"Carol's right," said Tori's father.

"*Carol* should mind her own business," spat Tori's mother.

Roger Arnold stepped forward and took Tori's mother's arm.

Tori's eyes darted back and forth among the four adults. So much for the great news, she thought. This was all wrong.

Tori's father wrinkled his brow. "I think we should talk about this, Tori," he said softly.

Tori felt her face reddening. This wasn't what she'd had in mind at all.

Her father looked back at her mother and shrugged his shoulders helplessly. "It seems pretty clear that you haven't discussed this with either one of us," he said. "And I think you owe your mom a little more consideration than that. Don't you?"

Mrs. Carsen was still fuming. Both Roger and Carol were quiet. Tori felt sick. She wished she hadn't said anything.

Just then Nikki raced up, obviously not noticing what was going on between Tori and her two sets of parents.

"Guess what?" she practically shouted as she shared the news. "My mom had her baby! I have a little brother! Isn't that the greatest?" Nikki had a big smile on her face.

The adults stood there uncomfortably as Nikki grabbed Tori's hands and danced around with happiness. Tori didn't say anything.

"Tori, what is it?" Nikki asked. "Is something wrong?"

Tori couldn't move. It was hard to see Nikki so happy when she felt so miserable and confused about her own family.

Then, just as she thought things could not get any worse, Tori heard her name announced on the PA system. It was her turn to skate!

14

Tori practically stumbled out of the waiting area and past Mr. Weiler as she approached the ice. The gleaming white rink spread before her in a blaze of light. There was a hush as she tried to collect her thoughts before her music began. She skated out to the center and raised her arms gracefully over her head, taking up her position. As she did, she caught Mr. Weiler's eye at rinkside. He nodded and gave her an encouraging smile.

As soon as the first strains of the *William Tell* Overture trumpeted over the loud speakers, Tori began with intricate footwork around the entire rink, mixing in some forward and backward spirals, before landing a tuck axel. She glided across the rink doing a spread-eagle, and then, picking up speed again, zoomed into a double dip. On her takeoff, she felt her right shoulder drop and over rotate. Losing her balance, she hit the ice. As she climbed quickly to her feet and struggled to catch up with the music, a wave of fear settled in her stomach. This was a nightmare!

But as the music continued and Tori sped across the rink with backward crossovers before coming to the double Lutz–double toe loop combination, she suddenly remembered what Mr. Weiler had said about having a good time while she was skating. She had to admit, it made her feel pretty good that her mother had come all the way from Montreal to see her skate.

She felt the music welling up all around her, and with a big smile she performed her double axel, smoothly leading to the double Lutz–double toe loop combination. Without missing a beat, she performed a flying camel spin and completed the footwork that blended beautifully with the pounding of the violins. Finally, smiling at the judges with her head held high, she ended with a dramatic series of Arabian cartwheels and flying splits, and closed with a final scratch spin, her arms and fingers fully extended in a triumphant sweep directly in front of the judges.

Tori caught Mr. Weiler's eye, and he smiled. She knew she would have performed much better if she had practiced more seriously, but at least she'd done better than in the short program the day before. Perhaps most importantly, she had been able to put aside her personal problems to skate as a competitor.

As her mother always said, grace under pressure was an important quality for a champion. Tori felt proud that she had not given up on herself.

She left the ice and headed to her mom and Roger, who were still standing a few feet away from her father and Carol, all of them still looking uncomfortable with each other. But all four of them were smiling proudly at her. Tori grinned back when she saw how pleased everyone was with her performance. After accepting hugs from everyone except Roger, Tori grinned at him and finally let him put his arm around her, too.

Then she took a step back and said, "Thanks, everybody. And I'm sorry about before." She turned to her father. "You're right, we have to talk."

"Yes, Tori," said her father.

"I'd like to speak with you, too, Tori," said her mother in a tight voice.

Looking at her mother's sad face, Tori felt a twinge of guilt. "I'm sorry, Mom," she said softly.

Her mother put her arm around her. "I understand," she said.

Tori gazed at her mother, then her father, then back to her mother, and suddenly it was all clear to her. Maybe her mom hadn't been around as much as she should have these past couple of weeks, but she was the one who'd been there for Tori for thirteen whole years. She and her mom were a team—a great team! Her mom had even shortened her trip to Montreal to watch Tori compete. And, as she studied her father's face, Tori realized she'd overreacted to his letter because she'd been angry with her mother. How could she possibly live with her father and Carol when they traveled all over the world half the year? She wasn't even sure she liked Carol. And she barely knew her father.

"I'm sorry, everyone," said Tori softly. "I made a mistake. A big mistake. My home is in Seneca Hills. With Mom."

Tori gave her mother another big hug, and Mrs. Carsen hugged her harder. Then Tori excused herself to change. She smiled at herself in the locker room mirror. Even though things were far from perfect, she was relieved to be going back to Seneca Hills.

Later, sitting with her father in the café, Tori was glad she could talk with him privately about why she had wanted to move to Lake Placid.

"I understand your feelings," her father said, "but you have to remember, your mom's always been there for you."

"I know," Tori agreed.

"Carol and I are still new at this parenting thing," he went on. "I don't know if we'd be ready to do it full-time, anyway. Besides, your mom loves you very much, and I would never want to interfere in your relationship with each other."

"You're right, Dad," Tori sighed. "I know I probably shook everyone up. I guess I wasn't thinking."

"Not that I'm not looking forward to spending
more time together," added Mr. Carsen. "I've often
thought since we met how much we have to make
up for. You can spend time with us in lots of ways.
But with your mom's approval."

"I know that's right. I guess I have a lot to make
up for with her, too," Tori admitted. "Thanks, Dad.
You've been great." Tori stood up and hugged her
father. "I'd better go and talk to Mom. I'll see you
and Carol later, okay?"

"Okay, Tori," her father said with a smile. "I'm
proud of you, champ."

Tori found her mother upstairs in the hotel room,
arranging Tori's clothes in her suitcase.

"I thought maybe you'd like to drive back with me
and Roger," said her mother. "Unless you'd prefer to
go with the other girls in the bus." Mrs. Carsen
looked a little sad and unsure as she put another
shirt into the suitcase.

"Mom," Tori said, taking her mother gently by the
arm and sitting down with her on the bed. "Mom, I
want to apologize to you. I shouldn't have gone behind your back like that." Tori swallowed hard. She
looked into her mother's face. "I guess I was upset
by how much attention you were paying to Mr. Arnold instead of me."

"Oh, Tori," her mother said, her face lighting up

with a smile. "No one will ever come between you and me, unless we let them. We're a team, remember? Teammates are *always* there for one another. I love you."

"I love you too, Mom," Tori said.

"Now, about your performance out there on the ice," her mother began. "Technically you weren't there at all, Tori. You could have placed in this competition if you'd set your mind to it."

"I know, Mom," sighed Tori. "I should have done better. I can't believe I came in tenth! I've never placed that low before."

"You certainly should have done better," her mother went on. "You lost to girls you could have beaten." Her mother paused, and her expression softened. "But I guess it's been hard for you these past couple of weeks. I'm sorry, too, I know I haven't done the best job of balancing everything out, but we'll work on it and soon things will be easier. You have to give us a chance. Especially with Roger. He's such a sweet man."

Tori made a face.

"Oh, come on," said her mother. "Give Roger a break. He really likes you."

"I don't see how he could," said Tori, shaking her head. "I haven't been very nice to him."

"No," Mrs. Carsen agreed with a smile, "you haven't been very nice, but he knows a sweetie when he sees one."

"Well, I can believe that," Tori retorted. "He sure knew what he was doing when he spotted you!"

They both laughed, and then Mrs. Carsen said, "But seriously, Tori, I don't understand how you could have let your practice go like that. You can do much better than you did today, and I know it. So do you. How are we going to decorate the living room with all your gold medals if your skating looks like that?"

Mrs. Carsen and Tori hugged, and Tori felt a million times better. She felt the happiest she'd been in weeks. Her mom was back on the Carsen team!

"Wow," Haley said as the girls approached Nikki's front door the following weekend. "They really did a great job on this monogramming." Her fingers traced the raised red letters on the ivory coverlet and pillow set the girls had bought for Nikki's new baby brother.

" 'B.E.S.,' " Tori read out loud. "I love his name. It sounds so classic. Benjamin Edwards Simon."

"Tori, I'm so happy you thought of this," Haley said. "We never would have been able to get something this nice if we hadn't gone to the big sale for the Arnold's store opening."

"I think the red looks great. Jill was right," added Danielle. "Red looks good with everything."

"It's very cheerful," Tori agreed. "And with everything half off, we got something twice as nice for our money."

"Yeah, that was great," said Haley, closing the box with the present inside. "Are we ready to go in?"

"Ready!" Danielle and Tori answered.

The girls knocked on the Simons' front door. Nikki answered with a big grin.

"Special delivery!" the girls said happily.

Nikki put a finger to her lips. "He's sleeping," she said quietly. "Come on in."

The girls tiptoed in and waved hello to Mrs. Simon. She was holding the sleeping baby close to her and folded back a corner of the blanket for the girls to see.

Tori gazed at the little bundle in Mrs. Simons's arms. With his tiny pink face and thin wisps of reddish brown hair, the baby was adorable.

"Can you believe it?" whispered Nikki happily. "Now we're a family of four. Isn't that great?"

"It sure is," said Tori. But a family of two can be pretty special, too, she added to herself.

#4: Going for the Gold

It's a dream come true! Jill's going to the famous figureskating center in Colorado. But the training is *much* tougher than Jill ever expected, and Kevin, a really cute skater at the school, has a plan that's sure to get her into *big* trouble. Could this be the end of Jill's skating career?

#5: The Perfect Pair

Nikki Simon and Alex Beekman are the perfect pair on the ice. But off the ice there's a big problem. Suddenly Alex is sending Nikki gifts and asking her out on dates. Nikki wants to be Alex's partner in pairs but not his girlfriend. Will she lose Alex when she tells him? Can Nikki's friends in Silver Blades find a way to save her friendship with Alex *and* her skating career?

#6: Skating Camp

Summer's here and Jill Wong can't wait to join her best friends from Silver Blades at skating camp. It's going to be just like old times. But things have changed since Jill left Silver Blades to train at a famous ice academy. Tori and Danielle are spending all their time with another skater, Haley Arthur, and Nikki has a big secret that she won't share with anyone. Has Jill lost her best friends forever?

#7: The Ice Princess

Tori's favorite skating superstar, Elyse Taylor, is in town, and she's staying with Tori! When Elyse promises to teach Tori her famous spin, Tori's sure they'll become the best of friends. But Elyse isn't the sweet champion everyone thinks she is. And she's out to make get Tori in *big* trouble!

#8: Rumors at the Rink

Haley can't believe it—Kathy Bart, her favorite coach in the whole world, is quitting Silver Blades! Haley's sure it's all her fault. Why didn't she listen when everyone told her to stop playing practical jokes on Kathy?

With Kathy gone, Haley knows she'll never win the next big competition. She has to make Kathy change her mind—no matter what. But will Haley's secret plan work?

#9: Spring Break

Jill is home from the Ice Academy, and everyone is treating her like a star. And she loves it! It's like a dream come true—especially when she meets cute, fifteen-year-old Ryan McKensey. He's so much fun and cool—and he happens to be her number one fan!

The only problem is that he doesn't understand what it takes to be a professional athlete. Jill doesn't want to ruin her chances with such a great guy. But will dating Ryan destroy her future as an Olympic skater?

THE SADDLE CLUB™

❏ 15594-6	HORSE CRAZY #1	$3.50/$4.50 Can.	❏ 15938-0	STAR RIDER #19	$3.50/$4.50 Can.
❏ 15611-X	HORSE SHY #2	$3.25/$3.99 Can.	❏ 15907-0	SNOW RIDE #20	$3.50/$4.50 Can.
❏ 15626-8	HORSE SENSE #3	$3.50/$4.50 Can.	❏ 15983-6	RACEHORSE #21	$3.50/$4.50 Can.
❏ 15637-3	HORSE POWER #4	$3.50/$4.50 Can.	❏ 15990-9	FOX HUNT #22	$3.50/$4.50 Can.
❏ 15703-5	TRAIL MATES #5	$3.50/$4.50 Can.	❏ 48025-1	HORSE TROUBLE #23	$3.50/$4.50 Can.
❏ 15728-0	DUDE RANCH #6	$3.50/$4.50 Can.	❏ 48067-7	GHOST RIDER #24	$3.50/$4.50 Can.
❏ 15754-X	HORSE PLAY #7	$3.25/$3.99 Can.	❏ 48072-3	SHOW HORSE #25	$3.50/$4.50 Can.
❏ 15769-8	HORSE SHOW #8	$3.25/$3.99 Can.	❏ 48073-1	BEACH RIDE #26	$3.50/$4.50 Can.
❏ 15780-9	HOOF BEAT #9	$3.50/$4.50 Can.	❏ 48074-X	BRIDLE PATH #27	$3.50/$4.50 Can.
❏ 15790-6	RIDING CAMP #10	$3.50/$4.50 Can.	❏ 48075-8	STABLE MANNERS #28	$3.50/$4.50 Can.
❏ 15805-8	HORSE WISE #11	$3.25/$3.99 Can..	❏ 48076-6	RANCH HANDS #29	$3.50/$4.50 Can.
❏ 15821-X	RODEO RIDER #12	$3.50/$4.50 Can.	❏ 48077-4	AUTUMN TRAIL #30	$3.50/$4.50 Can.
❏ 15832-5	STARLIGHT CHRISTMAS #13	$3.50/$4.50 Can.	❏ 48145-2	HAYRIDE #31	$3.50/$4.50 Can.
❏ 15847-3	SEA HORSE #14	$3.50/$4.50 Can.	❏ 48146-0	CHOCOLATE HORSE #32	$3.50/$4.50 Can.
❏ 15862-7	TEAM PLAY #15	$3.50/$4.50 Can.	❏ 48147-9	HIGH HORSE #33	$3.50/$4.50 Can.
❏ 15882-1	HORSE GAMES #16	$3.25/$3.99 Can.	❏ 48148-7	HAY FEVER #34	$3.50/$4.50 Can.
❏ 15937-2	HORSENAPPED #17	$3.50/$4.50 Can.	❏ 48149-5	A SUMMER WITHOUT HORSES Super #1	$3.99/$4.99 Can.
❏ 15928-3	PACK TRIP #18	$3.50/$4.50 Can.			

Bantam Doubleday Dell
Books For Young Readers

Bantam Books, Dept. SC35,
2451 South Wolf Road, Des Plaines, IL 60018   DA60

Please send the items I have checked above. I am enclosing $_____ (please add $2.50 to cover postage and handling). Send check or money order, no cash or C.O.D.s please.

Mr/Ms _____

Address _____

City/State _____ Zip _____

Please allow four to six weeks for delivery.
Prices and availability subject to change without notice.   SC35-4/94